"Meissner's stories blend the ironic edge of Raymond Carver and the poetic rhythms of Richard Hugo, using baseball as a touch point for life experiences."

LOS ANGELES TIMES

"For Meissner, baseball is a bulwark against change, against the painful, even tragic evanescence of life itself. The best stories in this collection express that feeling with great tenderness."

PUBLISHERS WEEKLY

"Meissner has a feel for both baseball's appeal and the people to whom it appeals. A lovely book."

BOOKLIST

"Bill Meissner is a baseball purist . . . a lyrical, accessible, and above all relevant collection."

THE COOPERSTOWN REVIEW

"A book that should be replayed from cover to cover for the end-of-the-year highlights. An MVP performance!"

JACK DRISCOLL

"Bill Meissner's fiction proves once again that in the hands of a sensitive, skilled and caring writer, baseball becomes a bridge between generations, connecting fathers and children and eliciting sentiments about life and its promise."

PETER LEVINE, AUTHOR OF A.G. SPALDING AND THE RISE OF BASEBALL

"There is much of value here, not only for the true baseball fan, but also for the true lover of quality short fiction."

DALLAS MORNING NEWS

"Just about every tale here recalls those precious years when a chance to play in the majors was all a boy could ask from life."

"Bill Meissner's baseball writings are major league material."

"Meissner writes less about how the game is played on the field than how it is lived in the heart. He is very good at this, as good as anyone I've ever read."

"Meissner's tales manage a dreamy, introspective lyricism."

"A quiet masterpiece of baseball writing . . . rich with poetic language and convincing characters."

"Meissner's stories are fully formed, haunting, and beautiful."

"You don't need to be a baseball fan to enjoy these poignant tales."

"Meissner's *Hitting into the Wind* isn't just good baseball fiction; it's good fiction, period."

Also by Bill Meissner

Learning to Breathe Underwater
The Sleepwalker's Son
Twin Sons of Different Mirrors (with Jack Driscoll)

Hitting into the Wind

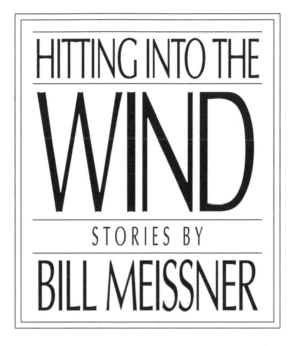

HITTING INTO THE
WIND

STORIES BY

BILL MEISSNER

SOUTHERN
METHODIST
UNIVERSITY
PRESS

Dallas

Requests for permission to reproduce material from this work
should be sent to:
  Rights and Permissions
  Southern Methodist University Press
  PO Box 750415
  Dallas, Texas 75275-0415

These stories were originally published in *Baseball History, Great
River Review, Indiana Review, Mid-American Review, The
Minneapolis Review of Baseball, Minneapolis Star-Tribune Sunday
Magazine, Minnesota Monthly, Nine: A Journal of Baseball History
and Social Perspectives,* and *Twin Cities Magazine.*

Library of Congress Cataloging-in-Publication Data

Meissner, William, date.
    Hitting into the wind / Bill Meissner. — 1st Southern
Methodist University Press ed.
        p.   cm.
    ISBN 0-87074-416-X (paper : alk. paper)
    1. Baseball stories, American.   I. Title.
    [PS3563.E38H57   1997]
    813'.54—dc21   96-51732

Cover illustration by Marc Burckhardt

Printed in the United States of America on acid-free paper
10   9   8   7   6   5   4   3   2   1

For Christine and Nathan,
always the best teammates.

Also for my mother, Julia Meissner, and in memory of my father,
Leonard Meissner, 1914–1988.

Acknowledgments

I would like to express my gratitude to the Loft-McKnight Foundation for a 1989 Loft-McKnight Award of Distinction in Fiction and to the PEN/NEA Syndicated Fiction Project for their continued support through five awards for my stories. In 1993, "Baseball Hands" was selected for a PEN/NEA award.

Thanks also to the Minnesota State Arts Board for a 1982 fellowship and to the National Endowment for the Arts.

I would like to thank the following publications, where these works appeared:

Minnesota Monthly: "Kirby Puckett's Legs: A Symphony in Nine Innings"

Minneapolis Star-Tribune Sunday Magazine: "Just Another Baseball Story," "The Unwinding," "Baseball, Fathers, and Dreams"

Twin Cities Magazine: "Hitting into the Wind" (reprinted in *The Minneapolis Review of Baseball*)

Mid-American Review: "The John F. Kennedy Wiffle Ball"

Indiana Review: "The Outfielder" (subsequently reprinted in the *Minneapolis Star-Tribune Sunday Magazine* and syndicated to six other publications through The Fiction Network of San Francisco)

Nine: A Journal of Baseball History and Social Perspectives: "Freight Trains, Flights of Geese, Shoes, and Homers: The

Whole Truth About the Journey of an American Baseball" and "A Song for Hank Aaron's Swing"

Baseball History: Portions of "Baseball Hands" (entitled "Rituals: The Oiling of the Glove")

Great River Review: "The Heaven of Baseball"

Contents

FOUR.   Leaning Toward the Dugout

ONE

Taking
the
Field

The Outfielder

1

What I like most is the room to move, room to flow until I'm under the high flies, waiting for their whiteness to cover my palm. There's a beauty in the outfield, a grace. Out here, no one touches you. You throw long pegs to second or home, but these are the only lines of connection. No one seems to know what I mean, to love it as much as I do. The woman I love understands it, but not completely. I try to tell her about it, but there are times when, like the flag stiffening on the center flagpole, she pulls away from me and doesn't want to listen.

2

The woman I love tells me, *Look out into the world. Look beyond yourself, your game.* I love her for saying that. If she didn't say things like that, I would never love her. Still, she doesn't really know what I mean by the beauty of the soft, cropped green outfield.

We drive in cars a lot. Sometimes she talks to me, sometimes she doesn't. She never talks outfield. She thinks I get enough of it during the games themselves. Sometimes she talks houses: kitchens, sunlight sliding through the slats in the blinds, homes. What we could have between us. She purposely avoids talking outfield. How I love that game.

Sometimes we stand in the kitchen and talk for hours. The floors are green and clean, and I brush my toe across the tiles. Sometimes we sit at a diamond-shaped table. Lifting my coffee to my lips, I look up at the walls. *Just don't let it be everything to you,* she says. I even love the *way* she says it: her strength, the way the words leap out at just the right moment.

3

She agrees with me when I say I'm lucky I'm not an infielder. Lucky I'm not a shortstop or third baseman, those guys who can take only three or four steps before they dive for the hard grounders. I can't stand the feeling of dirt beneath my cleats. Sometimes infielders are frozen by a line drive that, if it hit them, would shatter their bones like glass. I'm glad I'm not a catcher, held stiff behind mask and shin guards, a crouched crustacean. Glad I am not a pitcher, tearing my arm out by its roots while batters try to smack each pitch and bounce it off the moon.

Learn to be fast, I always told myself as a kid. *Never be slow, or they'll stick you in the infield.* I impressed them with the way my feet did not seem to touch the grass when I ran. Now, as a veteran, I must fight every day to keep my legs young.

4

Fans, she says, *are only superficial. They never love you the way I love you.* And I know it's true. She reminds me that the fans don't know the real me, don't see me in the mornings, dropping my peanut-butter toast to the kitchen floor. They have my photographs, touched up just right so they can't see the lines under my eyes. They don't see the chalky color of my face when I wake too early, my timing off.

The fans love me, in their way. And I love them. Sometimes the sound of their cheers is like pure sunlight in my ears. But the fans admire me only in my white pinstriped uniform in center field under the floodlights; they don't see my shadow. *I do,* she says, and her timing is just right as she rounds her lips to say the words, just like a practiced umpire saying, "Strike two." I stand up from my side of the table, brush her hair back with my glove hand, touch her cheek with my bare hand.

5

An outfielder has a certain liking for fences, walls. Walls seem to contain you better than open fields do. You might say I am a little in love with walls. They let you know your limitations, they speak strongly to your shoulders when you back into them. Sometimes they outline my life.

They stop those line drives between center and left that skip by too quickly for any human to reach. They send the ball careening off, skimming toward you, so you can barehand it and nail the runner trying to stretch it to third.

I love to play the wall. Sometimes the true test is holding on to the ball you've just caught, even though you've run full speed into the wall and everything hurts. The fences make the game.

A high fly to deep center excites me more than a pop-up that takes only a step or two to catch. I love the wait, my back to the fence, as the ball approaches, high and spinning with all its strength. I love it when the ball finally arcs down out of orbit. *Just out of reach,* everyone thinks. Then the leap. The stretching of tendons. And I come down with a smile of white leather in my web, so bright it stings the batter's eyes.

6

The night she left me, the outfield grass felt like crushed apples, crushed apples, crushed apples.

7

Timing is everything. It's knowing where you'll catch the ball even before the batter hits it. Timing is knowing when to dive for the line drive that's falling fast, it's knowing which shoestring catches to go for, which are out of range.

If I drop a fly ball, I'm the only one to blame. Infielders can bobble a grounder, still throw their man out. With an outfielder, it's decisive: The fly ball cannot touch the grass or I die a little, right there in front of everyone.

Timing is everything when you're growing old. It's knowing the loss of a wasted moment, feeling the pain as you let it drop just beyond your fingertips.

Last night I dreamt of my first baseball glove. I used it for years as a grade-school kid; it was a dark leather glove with swollen fingers and I eventually lost it somewhere in high school. In my dream I slipped the glove on and it felt too tight for my hand. When I tried to take it off, it wouldn't let go of my fingers. Suddenly the leather began to crack and flake. For those few agonizing seconds before the dream ended, I pulled and pulled but couldn't slide that glove from my hand.

Timing is thinking about this long, high fly ball hit to center, this deep one that's backing me toward the wall. Timing is understanding this last deadly instant, with its correct spring of leg muscles, its reach, its squeeze. Thinking about it, ready for it. Yes.

8

A game isn't a game unless it's a close game.

Sometimes, when I'm standing out there, toeing the grass,

watching man after man strike out or ground out, I think, *Let them get another run or two. Let them start some small fires.*

What good is playing if it's not hit for hit, run for run?

What does winning mean if you always win by half a dozen? What good is winning if you never lose? Closeness. Closeness is everything.

9

The score is tied after nine innings.

I turn around between pitches and see her in the center-field bleachers, watching me. Though she's never come to a game before, she's here; I can feel her eyes, like two heavy weights on my shoulders. Now's my chance to prove to her that I've never dropped one in my career, never.

This game lasts long into the night, until fans can see their breaths in the moist August air, and still the grass buoys up my cleats. *The beauty of it,* I think as I watch the next pitch, then turn to her, *the beauty.*

I can't see the stars, even though I know the sky is clear and endless. The bright floodlights build a wall between the stars and me. I know she understands the outfield, she wants to be out here with me. Her face is white and clean as a new baseball.

Another out, another run for our team and we can all go home. They'll turn off those huge rows of blindness and we'll see the heavens again, we'll see our faces clearly again, by touch.

I turn around once more and she's gone—there's only an empty hole in the bleachers where she sat. I can feel the lines etching deeper into my face, like grooves in the dirt of the dugout floor.

A hit rises from the batter's box. It's high and long to deep center. I race back at full speed, watching the ball over my shoulder all the while. The ball, a fleck of dust on the eye, begins its descent, and it appears that it's just out of reach. I time my leap.

Up. Full extension, my left arm stretched until all my muscles scream. The glove opens hungrily, lovingly for the ball. From this height I can see the stars again. The fans scream like sirens for me, and I think I hear her voice screaming for me, for the game, for the outfielder.

10

Back at home, we sit at the table in the green kitchen. We ignore all walls. She takes a sip of her coffee, then stands up. I stand up, slide around the table, and reach for her. With a pain that feels like flashbulbs popping behind my forehead, I catch her in my arms and she embraces me and we hold on. We hold on. To everyone's amazement, we hold on.

TWO

The Line
Drives of
Our Futures

Just Another
Baseball Story

That spring of freshman year, when the ball field at the edge of town exploded with grass brighter and greener than I'd ever seen it before, I played baseball. My best friend, Steve Lyon, and I practiced on that old West School field; all afternoon, we'd pitch and hit and field in the heat, until, around four o'clock, we'd cross the highway intersection to Kluge's gas station, sit on card-table chairs, and sip cold strawberry sodas. Sometimes we'd take off our ball caps and gaze at them, noticing where the sweat had evaporated from the bills in salty rings: pools of sweat, lakes of sweat, oceans of sweet sweat. The strawberry sodas always tasted great. Our shirts stuck to the metal chairs as, winded, we'd lean forward and stare at the paint-chipped wall. Without saying a word, we each knew what the other was thinking: Though we were only freshmen in high school, we were imagining chalk lines all the way to the majors.

We knew the major leaguer's yearning. It's that squint when there's no sun in the eyes. It's the eagerness for home runs, for diving catches, even though you're nothing more than a gawky kid, even though sometimes you feel lost, walking beneath an endless sky of splintered high school bleachers and rusting beams.

One afternoon that summer, when Steve was pitching to

me, he served up a fastball, and I hit that ball deep to left. It rose and kept rising over the tin roof of the two-story West School. We both stood and stared at it; Steve cheered in amazement as he watched it fly in an arc, disappear beyond the glinting silver roof.

While I slept that night, I saw the ball rising again. In the dream, Steve and I searched for hours in the uncut field behind the schoolhouse, but we never found it. Just before I woke up, Steve, who always told the truth, turned to me and said, "Forget it. It never came back to earth."

A few years ago, after college, I found a snapshot of myself in an attic drawer: I was on my first Little League team, and my face was squeezed and wrinkled from posing in the bright sun. As a kid, whenever I looked at that black-and-white photo, I saw myself in a red-and-white pro uniform. The sky-blue cap. The golden Louisville Slugger resting on one taut shoulder.

Last year, at Easter, we took a trip back to my hometown in south-central Wisconsin. Driving my six-year-old son past the old Broadway field, I told him that in Babe Ruth League, when I was sixteen, I hit a home run that flew beyond the grass embankment and over the sidewalk. It flew until it bounced high in the middle of the street, bounced all the way to the brick wall of Kluge's, where it ricocheted in the corner, where it sputtered and spun with dry leaves.

My son looked at me excitedly. He insisted that I drive around the block and pull over to the curb by the field, so I could tell him again just how far that home run had carried. As I retold the story, he traced an imaginary arc with his little finger between the distant backstop and Kluge's gas station. He believed the story, believed every word. And why shouldn't he, I thought; it *was* all true, wasn't it? I got out of the car and I strolled over to Kluge's; no one recognized me as I bought two cans of soda from the machine.

"Maybe it hit the edge of the grass first, now that I think of it," I admitted to him as I got back in the car.

"No," he assured me, sipping his strawberry soda. "It landed in the middle of the street."

The day I came home with my first Little League uniform, a purple Dodgers shirt, my dad walked me out to the backyard to take a picture. He snapped a black-and-white shot of me with the Brownie. In the fall, when we got the developed photos back from the drugstore, the picture turned out blurred, and my smeared face squinted into the sun. I frowned.

"I moved the camera," Dad explained. "I'm sorry. You looked a lot better."

In a desk drawer, I keep a frayed snapshot of my father on a championship team when he was in high school in Iowa. He once told me a story I never forgot: Before he got rheumatic fever, he hit a ball across the schoolyard where no one had hit it before, and it smashed through the second-story window of his grade school.

When I was six, we visited Dad's hometown in Iowa, and he drove us to his grade school. As we approached, he saw that a wide asphalt parking lot covered the city block where the school had once stood. He pulled the car to the curb and just sat there shaking his head, his hands clenching and unclenching the wheel. "It was here," he kept mumbling. "It was right here."

My son learned to hit a baseball this summer. I bought him a twenty-eight-inch bat for his birthday, and he's learning to watch the ball, to lean his small muscles into his swing as I pitch softly to him. Though he's so young, he's already developed his own style of batting, clenching and unclenching his fingers on the bat handle. The first time we played with a real baseball, he startled me by knocking a quick line drive straight at my chest.

The old West School was demolished during the seventies, and they tore down the backstop where Steve Lyon and I used to play. The infield area was smoothed over into a parking lot. Near the newly tarred highway, they built a Pizza Hut with a bright red plastic roof.

But we couldn't have known about that our freshman year; we just played baseball. We understood what we loved, and what we loved was permanent: the cracking of line drives, the diving for the tough ones just out of reach and coming up with grass stains on our elbows and white leather in our gloves.

We were crazy, everyone said. Crazy for the way we kept a record of how many hours we played baseball each summer. Crazy for playing ball one day in the middle of December, when snow covered the ground. Crazy to come home, laughing, delirious, tennis shoes and pant legs soaked from slogging across the melting snow toward a waterlogged ball. When we walked into the house, Dad asked us what we'd been doing. He just gave us a half-grin, half-grimace, and shook his head.

* * *

At the county fair the July after our freshman year, Steve and I spent a whole afternoon in a trailer exhibit called The Immortal Babe Ruth. We discovered the small Ruth exhibit on the midway; it drew few customers since it was sandwiched between the more popular side shows: Elastic Man and the Two-Headed Child. The Immortal Babe Ruth trailer was crammed with pictures and artifacts from the Babe's career, including his glove and his bats, and Steve and I lost ourselves in there for hours.

Later that August, my dad drove Steve and me to Milwaukee to see the Braves play. We were amazed by the skill of the players; sometimes it looked as though they'd never get under those high fly balls, as if they hardly cared, and then, suddenly, in one fluid motion, they were waiting beneath them, ready to snag the ball one-handed.

In the ninth inning, Hank Aaron hit what seemed to be a routine infield fly ball down the third-base line. We sat, our mouths gaped into ovals, as the ball just kept rising and rising until, by the time it came down, it had cleared the left-field fence at the 325 mark. When it hit the strip of asphalt beyond the fence, it bounced high into the air, as if it were beginning its ascent again.

At home in the evening, on my way upstairs to sleep, I noticed Dad pulling something out of a musty desk drawer. I looked over his shoulder and saw it between his fingertips: the picture of himself on the championship team back in Iowa. Without looking up at me, he said: "Once, when I was pitching, their best hitter hit a line drive right at my chest. But I caught the ball for the third out. It was coming back at me at a hundred miles an hour, but I caught it." I looked again at the picture he held carefully between his fingertips. He was much thinner, standing there in the front row, and I could see his face clearly: A smile slid across it, and it wasn't blurred, wasn't blurred at all.

The next day, he asked me to put on my freshman team uniform and walk into the backyard for a picture. I noticed him puffing a little as he carried his weight up the gentle incline. Even back then, he admitted he was having chest pains every once in a while. "Right here," he said, and he had me stand in the shade of the oak tree, so I wouldn't squint. I just stood there self-consciously with the bat.

"No, no," he said. "Crouch in your batting stance. As if you're about to hit a home run." He tossed his cigarette to the grass, rested the Brownie on his stomach, stared into the viewfinder, and steadied himself as he backed up a few steps on the hillside. Then he took a deep breath, held it, and clicked the shutter. "Perfect," he said. "This one'll turn out perfect."

When Steve and I went back to the county fair the summer after sophomore year, the Babe Ruth exhibit was gone. In its place was the Ghost Child—Born Without Eyes or Ears, the sign told us. *Unbelievable,* all the kids said—*you have to see it.* After some deliberation, Steve and I finally paid our quarters for the Ghost Child. The child, floating in a large jar filled with formaldehyde, looked as though it were made of plastic. "Not real," we said later—"a stupid fake." And we quickly forgot about it. What we talked about on the way home was the Babe Ruth exhibit, and the Babe's Yankee uniform, which looked crumpled and gray like the skin a snake might have shed.

*   *   *

When we visited my hometown last Easter, my son said he was hungry for a pizza. So I drove him to the Pizza Hut at the edge of town. I pulled into the parking lot, stepped out of the car, and stood there a moment, looking down at the asphalt.

My son got out of the car and squinted at me. "What, Daddy?" he finally asked.

"Home plate," I told him. "We're standing on home plate."

Tonight my son finds my old scrapbook in the attic. We page through it, looking at yellowed newspaper clippings whose brittle corners crumble to the touch.

The old photo of my father's team slips from between the black pages and flutters to the floor. My son looks at the player circled in the front row.

"Who's that?" he asks. "You?"

"No," I answer. "That was Grandpa."

On the next page, we come upon that photo Dad took of me in my freshman uniform. They underexposed it at the drugstore—the picture was so dark, it looked like it was taken at night, and you couldn't even see my face beneath the shadow of my cap's brim. Dad said to save the picture anyway.

We close the album, and I begin to tell my son about Steve and me, about our years of baseball.

"Why'd you stop playing?" my son wants to know.

I fall silent for a few seconds. I can't explain it to him. Maybe I should tell him that the dreams somehow changed beneath us, like vivid summer grass gradually drying in the fall. Or maybe it was like standing in a field as dusk begins to surround you. But he's too young to understand that. Nor would he understand a story about the last time I saw Steve.

Senior year in college, during semester break, I noticed

Steve sitting in a darkened bar, the Saturday ball game blaring on the TV in the far corner. I sat down next to him on a red vinyl stool. We both held half-finished glasses of beer. We talked a little about college, about summer jobs, classes, credits. Then we both admitted we hadn't touched a baseball in years. He smiled, lit a cigarette, drew a deep drag from it, and shrugged. We used to be crazy, we both agreed.

We reminisced about our grade-school and high-school days. "Remember that great catch in the championship game?" we said. "Remember that hit? Remember Aaron's homer?" Each time we spoke, the ball flew a little higher in our minds. After a while, we paused, held still for a moment in the flickering light of the black-and-white TV. None of it seemed true anymore. We clutched our beer glasses, lifted the warm edges to our lips.

For a few moments, neither of us said anything, but we each knew what the other was thinking. We were thinking back to late August of freshman year, when we sat in Kluge's gas station after a long afternoon of baseball. We saw ourselves lean back on card-table chairs, stare straight ahead— beyond the paint-chipped walls—toward the beautiful line drives of our futures. That cold strawberry pop was always too sweet on our tongues. But we loved the taste, and we drank it, we drank it all.

The John F. Kennedy
Wiffle Ball

It didn't matter that the wind seemed to blow my high pop-ups across my yard and back to home plate. It didn't matter that the stiff weeds down the third-base line sometimes stopped a hard line drive cold. What mattered was that when I'd hit the Wiffle ball, its surface covered with evenly spaced holes, it would make that high-pitched fluttering sound as it cut through the air above my yard. What mattered was that one afternoon in 1961, the spring after Kennedy was elected, I knelt in the middle of the diamond with a black Magic Marker and wrote the initials JFK on my new Wiffle ball.

The day before, I had ceremoniously lowered a linoleum square home plate beneath the birch tree at the back corner of the yard and punched sticks into the ground down the third- and first-base lines for foul markers, and my small backyard was transformed into a major league stadium. Bleachers appeared in the tarred street in left, and I could hear the crowd buzzing, like cicadas, for the start of the game. I played a nine-inning game pitch by pitch, calling balls and strikes, tossing the Wiffle ball into the thin branches of the elm just above home plate and swinging at it with a wooden bat. I'd swing and swing and swing at the ball for hours on summer afternoons, not caring about the time my uncle said I wasted. Sometimes I had the feeling that my whole life was right there in that backyard, that nothing else in the world existed except me and my Wiffle ball stadium.

Like a lot of young boys, I was alone with my game. I was quiet, and baseball was my best friend, the one friend I could be myself with. Once in a while, I pictured, across town, other small boys in their backyards, playing imaginary baseball just like me. Sometimes, during my best games, I pictured half a million boys across America in their backyards, playing Wiffle ball and imagining.

Before each swing, I watched the initials JFK rotate in the soft air. The JFK ball always seemed to fly farther than my other, everyday Wiffle balls. I didn't use it often, but saved it for special occasions or important play-off games.

In dead center, the home-run line was the sidewalk, the farthest point in my stadium. During my games, no one, not Henry Aaron, not Ted Williams, not mighty McCovey of the Giants, had hit one out in center. It was no man's land. It was The Wall. I used to imagine it out there: ten feet high, brick. I sometimes thought of moving center a little closer by setting a box or the garden hose in the grass, but I never did. In my whole career in the Wiffle ball stadium, which lasted two years, I never hit one out in center. It was unreachable with a Wiffle ball, unless a gust of wind caught the ball and lifted it higher than I could ever have hit it. Still, I kept trying.

On Saturday afternoons I took the small beige transistor radio into the yard with me, put it on a tree stump, and played my Wiffle game, inning by inning, along with the live action of a pro game. Sometimes, during the news spots on the hour, I heard Kennedy speaking to me. I often heard him on the nightly news as I sat with my aunt and uncle eating dinner on our TV trays. I saw Kennedy talking into a microphone covered with holes, telling us that America would become fit and strong, and we wouldn't stop until we reached the moon. I believed him. I believed that no matter how old you were, when Kennedy spoke, you had faith, and you were young again. Kennedy always seemed to speak of the future, of what was ahead, and sometimes I gazed far out into center field for a moment and I dreamed. I knew the future was out there somewhere, like a Wiffle ball rising and rising until it broke through the earth's atmosphere and went into orbit.

In our grade-school room, beneath the flag, was a picture of Kennedy next to the wall map of the United States. When I pledged allegiance I sometimes stared into his young eyes. I remember my class writing letters to him, congratulating him on the election. Those years I lived with my uncle, a staunch Republican who had worked for the Nixon campaign. When I came home from school and told him about the letters, he scowled disapprovingly. "What kind of class project is that?" he muttered, puffing on a chewed cigar.

I shrugged.

"What are you getting involved in politics for anyway?" he asked. "You're just kids."

Part of my fun with the Wiffle game was the sound effects. When I batted for my heroes, Hank Aaron or Eddie Mathews, and they'd hit a home run, I'd drop the baseball bat, cup my hands around my mouth, and exhale from my throat, imitating the sound of a whole stadium roaring.

Once Aaron hit the Wiffle ball deep to left center; it landed well beyond the concrete curb, a long homer, winning the game. The fans went wild and I imitated their two-minute roaring ovation. Hank Aaron took off his Milwaukee Braves cap and bowed. Suddenly I turned and noticed my uncle. He stood there with the garden hose coiled around his arm; his glare, threatening as a missile, was aimed right at me.

Stunned and embarrassed, I stopped my cheering, pulled

my hat on, and dropped my cupped palms awkwardly to my sides.

"What the heck are you doing?" he asked, taking one step toward me with his stocky legs, legs that had never played a day of baseball.

"Nothing," I said, lowering my gaze as if I were counting the thousand grass blades.

"What do you mean, nothing?" he demanded. "What was that supposed to be?"

"Cheers," I muttered.

"What?"

"Cheering," I explained. "A crowd cheering."

"Holy smokes," he said, shaking his head. "You and this game."

I stuffed my hands in the pockets of my blue gym shorts as the silence wrapped around me.

"I was watching you from the porch," he said, "and you know what I thought? *Nuts*, I thought to myself. My nephew's going *nuts*."

I couldn't find any words to respond. I felt my face igniting. Finally I bowed my head and uttered the only words I could: "It's just Wiffle ball."

"I don't care what you call it," he said, his voice gravelly, angry. "All this make-believe business. And this cheering. I don't want you cheering for yourself. You think you're some kind of hero, or what?"

I didn't respond, and he held the coil of plastic hose toward me. "Here," he said. "We've got work to do. Look at the dirt spots you're wearing into this lawn. The grass needs some seeding and watering. And your aunt wants the garage cleaned."

"Okay," I said, grabbing the hose, happy to move out from under his focus.

As he strode toward the faucet, he spotted something in the

grass. He picked it up. "What's this?" he asked, pointing to the JFK written on the ball.

I wished the yard would open up and swallow me.

"Whose initials are these supposed to be? Kennedy's?"

I just shrugged.

He shook his head. "For crying out loud," he said, and he tossed the ball over his shoulder. It caught and swayed in the stiff, spiked branches of the bushes along the first-base line.

UNBREAKABLE, the Wiffle balls said in tiny letters on their labels. GUARANTEED UNBREAKABLE. Yet, every few weeks, after I'd bounced one of my everyday balls off the big oak tree or the gray wall in right, the ball would begin to show hairline cracks in its white surface between the holes. The cracks would enlarge and soon they'd spread to two or three holes, so that when you hit the ball on that side it would collapse for an instant and not fly like it should. When that happened, I'd march down to the Ben Franklin store, show them the label and my receipt for fifty-nine cents that I'd kept in my dresser drawer, and ask for a new Wiffle ball. Then I'd stroll home proudly, tossing the new ball into the air. I knew my rights; it was the American way. After a few trips to the hardware store, I could tell Mr. Wendt was beginning to get irritated. "What are you doing with these things?" he asked one time when I brought in yet another cracked ball. "Using them for target practice?" I just shrugged, held out the ball, and he reluctantly reached to the shelf and handed me a new one.

During that year I heard news about how, in Berlin, Germany, they were building a huge brick-and-stone wall. I heard they put barbed wire on top of it, just to keep in the

East Berliners. Kennedy spoke out against it, said it was wrong to lock people in, to keep them from freedom. Sometimes, when Kennedy spoke, I believed it was America speaking to me.

That night I dreamt of hitting the JFK Wiffle ball so deep to center that it cleared the Berlin Wall for a home run. The fans leaped to their feet to shout and celebrate, their arms waving, waving like the wind rippling across endless grassy fields.

I always used a heavy wooden bat when I played Wiffle ball because my friends said it would make you stronger. Keep swinging it, they said, and it'll build your arm muscles. But after a whole season of swinging, I stood in front of the bedroom mirror without my shirt and looked at my bony, sunken chest, looked at my wrists: thin, the tendons showing like brittle wires. "A birch twig," my uncle once muttered as he walked past the doorway and saw me, standing there bare chested. "You'll never be a baseball player when you're built like a birch twig." Still, I kept picturing myself at seventeen or eighteen, arms like Mantle, arms strong enough to hit a ball all the way to the moon. Other times, peering into the mirror, I thought maybe my uncle was right. Maybe I *was* touched in the head. Or maybe I imagined too much, a hopeless dreamer. Maybe all the kids across the country who played imaginary baseball were just hopeless dreamers.

In 1963, when Kennedy was shot, we all heard about it that morning at school. The news buzzed through the tiny holes in the tin loudspeakers on the wall, where our principal's voice had just listed the day's lunch menu. Our teacher sat down at her desk and dabbed her eyes with a Kleenex. A few minutes later, when she began talking again, I didn't listen. Instead, for the next hour, I just stared at the wall, at the map of the United States. As I stared, I thought I saw hairline cracks appearing on the surface of America. I kept staring, and thought I saw the cracks spread, intersecting and deepening.

At home, my uncle sat in the living room, which was dim except for the flickering light from the black-and-white Motorola.

He turned toward me when I walked in. "You heard?" he asked.

I nodded.

"I never agreed with the man," he said, his voice softened, almost hoarse. "Never really liked him. But they didn't have to shoot him."

The next day—an overcast Saturday with a blustery, numbing wind—most of us sat in our darkened living rooms and watched the reports on the television, watched the repeating film clips of the motorcade, watched the president slump in the seat, watched Jackie crawling out on the trunk of the car in her blood-spattered dress, watched the tearful interviews of parade spectators in Dallas. They called him a national hero. All three of us sat in the room, my aunt weeping on the stuffed chair, my uncle on one end of the couch, me on the other, none of us saying much. We sat so close together in that room, and so far apart.

All day, I couldn't shake the sensation that something had broken deep inside me. It was as though it had physically

snapped, like small, brittle cartilage or bone. And maybe
something had broken deep inside all the young boys in town.

The future was still out there. But I and the other boys
across America who played imaginary baseball didn't know
that for some of us, the future had changed. We didn't know
that after high school graduation, instead of walking down
the path to some bright stadium, we'd step out into the
shadowed green foliage of Vietnam, swinging M16's instead
of Louisville Sluggers as we followed tangled trails unmarked
by chalk lines or fences. We didn't know that for some of us,
the game would end quickly, mercilessly, like when a menac-
ing pitcher throws a hard one at you, and no matter how you
try, you can't get out of the way. Then it strikes you square
between the eyes and the last thing you know is your skull
exploding with darkness.

In late afternoon of that November day in '63, when my
aunt was in the kitchen making supper, I looked over and saw
my uncle, asleep on the couch in the living room. I tiptoed
over to turn down the volume on the TV, and I studied him.
He was putting on weight, and his rounded chest rose and fell
methodically. His balding head was tilted back on the padded
armrest and his mouth was slightly open. The wrinkles on his
face deepened in the shadow and light of the flickering images. He couldn't help it that he was old, I decided, and that
he was angry inside.

I couldn't bear to watch the news reports anymore, so I
walked out the back door in my white short-sleeved T-shirt.
"Where're you going?" my aunt asked, but I couldn't push
out a word to answer her. I picked up my wooden bat and a
cracked Wiffle ball in the garage, walked slowly toward home
plate. I stood there a moment and looked around. For some

reason, the backyard seemed smaller. It was just a yard with an oak tree, just a plot of browning grass cut off by the uneven sidewalk and the wall of our house. It was a yard, a small yard in a small town, and I was a small boy with scrawny wrists and gangly arms. There'd be no raspy cheering today. I braced myself in the gusts, my pant legs wrapping and unwrapping around my skinny ankles like flags.

I gazed out toward the farthest point of my stadium. Then I looked farther, to the rows of houses down our street, their picture windows bluish from the glowing television sets inside their living rooms, looked beyond the houses to the highway that led to the edge of town, looked far off, as if I could see all the way across America, though I realized, at that moment, I couldn't.

Then I lowered my eyes to the ball in my cupped palm, saw the fading initials JFK, heard the holes whistling slightly from the wind blowing so hard toward home. UNBREAKABLE, the label said. Gazing into the distance of center field, I tossed the ball high into the air and swung with all my strength.

A Bird, a Stone,
and Something Else

I've never been able to tell this story. It's a story about a bird, a stone, and a third thing, which I've never quite understood.

The summer of third grade, my buddies from Little League and I were sitting on a porch step with nothing to do, and one of the guys had an idea. He said we should hunt for birds with stones. Because we were eight years old, and because it was a long, boring August afternoon, and because the kid who thought up the idea was Dart Calley, the star pitcher and captain of our Little League team, we agreed to do it. Dart was tall for his age, a wiry, sneer-faced kid who always kept his Pirates cap pulled low on his forehead. He was a year older than the rest of us guys and could throw a pretty good fastball; he told us that sometimes he dusted off the batters in Little League on purpose, just to scare them. "What are we waiting for?" Dart asked as we stood, blinking at him. "Let's go get 'em."

So we gathered some stones from the edge of the garden behind my house and began our hunt. Though any kind of bird would do, except for the robin, which was our Wisconsin state bird, we decided to hunt blackbirds because we didn't like them—Dart told us his dad said the birds were no-good scavengers. Squeezing a rock in my fist, I followed the guys as we walked up and down the alley. The muscles in my arm were taut wires. Though my throws in Little League were usually high, arcing, and rainbow-shaped, the coach still remarked to my father that I had a "good wing" for a kid my age. By the end of that afternoon, we'd thrown a few rocks at birds perched on posts, but none of us had hit one.

During the next few days, we sometimes hunted as a group, but as time passed we began to split up—one or two of us might crouch in the weeds near the alley, while another one hid in the brush by the vacant lot and someone else stalked the birds in the fields across the street. By the second week, we began camouflaging our faces with black and green greasepaint—the stuff we smeared on our cheeks when we played war in the vacant lots with plastic guns. One afternoon a neighbor man walked through the field within ten feet of us and didn't even know we were there.

Just before five o'clock, or "seventeen hundred hours," as Dart called it, we met back at our headquarters, which was a stump in the corner of the field with a NO TRESPASSING sign nailed to it.

"Anything?" Dart would question as each kid reported in.

"Nothing," we'd say.

Then Dart would spread a wrinkled paper map on the dry stump and we'd plan our next day's strategy.

As the weeks passed, no one, not even Dart, ever came close to hitting a bird. As soon as the birds noticed us approaching, they'd hop nervously. It seemed that the very instant we'd raise our arms to throw, they'd burst into the air and flutter out of range. As the weeks passed, I began to think that this was a game we played just for the fun of the hunt, a game where we'd just go through the motions every day. After all, we were nothing more than kids with stones.

One humid afternoon in late August, when we stood talking by my garage, a big blackbird swooped over the backyard and landed at the edge of the grass by the alley. The bird stood there boldly, its feathers giving off a greenish iridescent sheen in the sunlight, its head tilting left, then right as it searched for insects.

Instinctively, I knelt near the garden and picked up a smooth, round, bluish-colored stone, about half the size of a baseball. The bird seemed beyond my range for accuracy; it was at least sixty feet from me even after I took a couple steps closer to it. I bent forward, paused, and watched it tilting its head left, then right.

I drew my arm back with the rock in my hand, and then something held it there, motionless.

"What're you waitin' for, stupid?" Dart hissed at me from behind. "Fire the rock. Fire the rock."

The bird hopped on its springing legs. It turned its back to me, tilted its head to one side, and stayed in that position a few seconds, as if it had spied an insect in the grass.

"Fire the damn rock," the voice insisted.

I threw the rock as hard as I could. It spun as it rode the straight line my eye had drawn between my hand and the bird. The rock struck the bird directly in the middle of its back with a *thunk*.

The bird's wings opened slightly with the impact, as if it were ruffling its feathers in the wind, and then, without a sound or a struggle, it simply tipped from its spindly legs and dropped onto its side. I ran up to it, still not believing I'd actually hit it. I felt the adrenaline throbbing in my arteries; I heard my friends' excited cries as they gathered in a circle around the bird and me.

I knelt down in the grass. The bird was still alive.

I looked into its eye—it was open wide, a round black glass

bead, staring at me, seeing its first human up close. For a few seconds, it seemed to be staring all the way to the back of my skull. Then, slowly, an opaque sheath slid over the eye from top to bottom like a window shade being pulled down, and the bird was dead.

It was the first living thing that ever died in front of me, and I saw it up close. There was no struggle, no blood. It just died, right there in my vision. It was that quick. It was that easy.

The more I think about it, the more I wonder why I haven't been able to tell about this before. Though I tried to stop it from replaying, I've had visions of the incident at least once a year for the twenty-some years since it happened. Of all people, I should be able to tell this story clearly.

After the bird died, the guys shouted victory cries and laughed and slapped me on the back. "Great throw!" someone exclaimed. "Way to go!" But for some reason I didn't feel like celebrating; my arm hung limp at my side. Without a word, I turned and walked quickly across the yard to my house.

"Hey, where you goin'?" Dart called toward my back. "Where the heck you goin'?"

Late that night, unable to sleep, I kept seeing my arm swing down hard, hurling that rock. I saw the rock, tumbling over and over itself in slow motion like a tiny planet lost in space, like the earth. I heard the sickening *thunk* as the rock hit the bird squarely in its back. I kept seeing that blackbird's eye— until the opaque lid slid over it, it was shiny, like the polished obsidian in my rock collection. That night I got out of bed, stood in front of my bedroom window, lifted the shade, and looked out at the yard, where the grass seemed stained with darkness. That night I kept thinking how the last thing that bird saw clearly before it died was me, leaning close to it. The last thing it saw was the enormous face of the human who killed it.

I never hunted birds again. I didn't join the guys in the alley after the ball games when they gathered, stones in their hands. Instead, if I felt like throwing rocks, I'd go down by the woolen mill near the river and take target practice at tin cans perched on fenceposts. Once, picking up a can I'd punctured with a rock, I cut my index finger on an edge of sharp, feathered tin. I watched that trickle of blood spiraling around my finger.

Near the end of that summer, just before school started again, I saw Dart Calley at Shogren's Grocery soda fountain, where a lot of grade-school kids hung out.

"Hey," Dart said as he chewed on a handful of Nibs, "how come you don't hunt birds with us no more?"

"Don't know," I answered.

"That was a great throw when you hit that blackbird," he exclaimed. I saw the candy, black between his teeth as he smiled.

"No it wasn't," I replied.

"Man," he said with a laugh, missing my tone, "did you see that thing die?"

"Yeah," I said, the word going flat on my tongue.

So that's the story about a bird, a stone, and a third thing. I know I've probably left out a lot of details. Over the years, I've learned that when it comes to a memory, the telling is always flawed, and somehow we never cover the *whole* story. After all, it's the incident itself, the moment frozen in time that holds its own pure truth, and all we can do is try to understand it, to explain it as best we can.

Perhaps now I can stop seeing that rock rotating in the air, stop seeing that glossy eye, and the opaque sheath slowly covering it. Perhaps now, rubbing the muscle of my arm, I can take the time to wonder: Is it how fast or accurately you throw, or is it throwing in the right direction that counts? Perhaps now I can jog to a baseball field, lie on my back in the grass, and gaze kindly at the blackbirds that always seem to be hovering overhead.

Water

If you've ever ridden on a team bus for nine hours toward Medicine Hat or Great Falls, as I have, you'd know what I mean. If you've ever followed that dry, straight road to a sun-bleached Wichita ball field and back, you'd understand. You'd understand what distance is, and what it means to a minor leaguer. You'd understand what the drive's like—beneath the floorboards, it's that steady droning sound, and ahead, through the bus's dust-caked windshield, all you can see is an endless mirage of shallow water that keeps pulling farther and farther away. No matter how many miles you drive, you never seem to catch up to it.

If you understood this, you'd understand a minor leaguer's yearning for water. You drive through lakeless states, drive in a tin bus that heats up like an oven across the parched fields of the Dakotas, where there's not even scrub brush for shade. You keep seeing, outside the oval side windows, the empty bowls of dried watering holes like blind eye sockets in the land. You're always by yourself on the bus, even if a buddy is sitting in the seat next to you. Even if he mutters to you now and then, or even if you play a hand of cards, you're always alone.

If you knew all this, and more, you'd understand why each night, after a ball game on some crippled field where the outfield grass is piled with gopher mounds, after a game where my socks are decorated with burrs that needle my ankles, after a game where my sweaty jersey clings to my skin like it'll never let go, after a game like that, I dream of water.

I dream of my small hometown back in Wisconsin, dream of riding in a sleek aqua Fairlane convertible with my girl-friend Melissa through the downtown, past the theater where we used to neck in high school, to the lake a mile outside town. The lake water is deep, everyone says; it's the deepest lake in the state. There are even Indian legends about the dark green drop-offs along the lake bottom. I dream of step-ping my bare feet slowly into that water off the steep rocky shoreline, dream of that cool water rising as I lower myself onto a submerged rock slab, slippery with algae. I dream of Melissa, facing me, wearing that bright blue two-piece, low-ering herself into the water, too, as she stares straight into my eyes. The spring-fed lake water's not too cold. It's never too cold. She lowers herself and the water rises to her waist, to her smooth breasts, to her slim, long neck. I watch the woman I love sliding into the liquid and I always think: *Water that touches her everyplace touches me everyplace.* This thought keeps flowing over and over in my mind as her blond hair swirls on the surface of the water around her bare shoulders. I submerge myself to my chin and feel the ripples from the water lapping at my face. She leans toward me and I lean toward her, and we're about to kiss, a deep, long, moist kiss, the kind of kiss that could last for years.

Then I wake up. I always wake up at that instant just before our lips touch. I wake up on a dry white sheet in some motel room on the road and it all comes back to me: I'm on the minor league circuit, six hundred miles from home. No way can I touch her lips.

Tonight I have the dream, and I wake up, and then something strange happens. I sit up and try to picture Melissa's face, her lips, but I can't. Like that water mirage on the highway, the harder I try to reach it, the farther away her face seems to be.

I stumble to the small desk lamp, click the light on, and pick up the phone. It bugs my roommate and I see him glare from his pillow, his face pinched like a fist, then grunt and roll over.

I dial her number. In the split second after I finish dialing, there's a hiss in the receiver before the connection, and I picture the electricity flowing through the thin black wires across the darkness of these arid flatlands, flowing from telephone pole to cracked telephone pole to Wisconsin, where streams rush through backyards, where the lawns are green. The phone rings once, twice, three times. When she answers, her words are groggy, sleep still coating her voice.

"Closer," I hear myself saying. "I want you closer."

"Denny?" she says. "What's wrong? Is anything wrong?"

"Yeah," I say. "We're wrong. You're at home and I'm here in some crummy motel in Kansas."

"Do you know it's three-fifteen in the morning?"

"I don't care what time it is," I say. "Jesus, Melissa, I miss you. I want you out here."

"You know I can't," she explains softly. "You know I can't leave my job."

I suddenly feel foolish for calling. I know she'd never come out here, and it's impossible for me to go back there. So what's the point of waking her up?

"The end of the season's not far off," she says, her voice trying to soothe me like liniment. "We can make it until then, can't we?"

"Not far off?" I say. "September's two months away."

"It's not forever," she says.

"It's a million years to me." I feel like there's sand in my throat when I say the words.

"I know. I know," Melissa says, her voice trailing off a little. "This isn't exactly easy for *me,* either."

The way she says this bothers me, and I pause for a few seconds, thoughts rushing through my head. I have a feeling things are going to be rocky when I get back. Before I met her, she had other boyfriends in town, and I know with me gone they wouldn't mind asking her out. I wish I could feel more sure about her. It's been so long since I've seen her, we'll hardly know what to say, how to look into each other's eyes. I picture her with a nervous half-smile, leaning on a wooden pillar on her front porch, twirling a small lock of her blond hair by the side of her face. I picture myself, my hands uncertain what to do, so they hide in my jeans pockets.

I finally break the pause. "Been to the lake lately?" I know it's a dumb thing to ask, but it's the only thing that comes into my mind.

"Lake?" Her voice rises, puzzled.

"Yeah. You know, swimming."

"Well, a few weeks ago. But not lately."

"Don't go. Not until I get home, I mean. That's the first place we'll go when I get back."

"Well . . . okay. If that's what you want." She laughs lightly, and when she laughs, it makes me think of ripples on the surface of water. I want to swim in those ripples.

I think about saying goodbye and hanging up the phone and I miss her already. That's the strange thing about being in the minors. You get a chance at something you love, but you always have to give up something else. There's a balancing in this life, a strange balancing, and sometimes it gets to a point where you just have to choose, because things don't stay balanced for long. It occurs to me that maybe I'm just thinking too much; sometimes the guys laugh at me and poke me with an elbow and say I'm thinking too much. Melissa and I talk a few more minutes, and before I hang up, I balance the black receiver in my hand.

The next day the team's on the road, and it's getting close to evening. One thing you learn in the minors is patience. Patience. You learn not to think more than a day ahead, or it will practically kill you. I met guys like that in Class A ball. They always talked about getting to the big leagues. *The Show*, they called it, as if they were going to appear on Johnny Carson or something. As if their whole life was spent hiding behind a thick curtain, being nobody, and then they'd get to The Show, where, all of a sudden, they were *somebody* in the spotlight. I wanted to tell them, *Hey, you are somebody. You're somebody now. Just be yourself. Just appreciate it.* But guys like that would have just scoffed and spat out their tobacco and turned their backs to me. The truth is, guys like that didn't last long. Guys like that thought too far ahead, as if their minds jumped years ahead of their bodies, which were still sitting on the slashed beige vinyl seat of a team bus, feeling each jolting pothole in a county highway. Guys like that went slowly crazy, saw their averages dwindle to nothing, swatted at batted balls with their gloves and came up empty. Guys like that threw their arms out on plays at the plate and you saw them after the game, pacing at the end of the bench, a bag of ice on their shoulders, talking to themselves. "Goddamn arm," they might be saying. "How the hell am I gonna make it to The Show now?"

We won't reach our next stop for a long time. Some of the guys on the bus are snapping cards on the slippery armrests.

Some talk in low voices and chuckle softly. Some sigh and write letters home.

But me, I'm just fingering the frayed hole in my jersey as I stare out the window through the reflection of my face in the glass. I'm staring at the small towns we drive through, one just the same as the next. I'm staring at the junk cars parked on the front lawns and the kids running free along the sidewalks. There's a small, scrubby baseball field with the silhouettes of the outfield floodlights on wooden posts, like crosses on the dusky horizon. Ahead of the bus, the sun sets and the road quickly darkens. I imagine, somewhere on the other side of the world, the sun rising, the water mirages just beginning on the roads, those mirages always just out of reach.

I'm thinking about things most ballplayers don't think about, I know, but I think about them anyway. I'm thinking about my girlfriend and me, and how time is passing each day, like something being pulled out from under us, and we don't even know it. We'll just look up one day and we'll be older, our hair splashed with gray, and we'll think back on these days. "Remember when you used to travel with that team?" she might say. And I might reply, "A million years ago. A million years."

But maybe I'm thinking too far ahead. So I pull my thoughts back a bit closer to where I am.

I'm staring out the window and thinking about my first day back from the minors, about how I'll jump into the battered Fairlane convertible with the woman I love and cruise through the downtown, past the theater with the unlit marquee bulbs and toward the lake. Two months is not too far to think ahead. Two months is just right. When we get to the lake, I'll grab Melissa's hand, pull her out of the passenger's side, and without even closing the door we'll run toward all that cool liquid that's been waiting for us.

It's night now, and we pass another small town; in one house, through a big picture window, I get a glimpse of the husband and wife, facing each other across the dinner table. As the window clicks past, they sit unmoving, frozen in the blue glow from the television set. There could be a ball game on. Or maybe it's a Johnny Carson special. Or maybe they don't even care what show's on, and all they're thinking about is looking deep into each other's eyes.

I hear the last few murmurs of conversation as the guys on the bus gradually run out of talk, and though it's way too early, I think about sleep. I think about dreaming. About things ballplayers never think about. A million years go by. I stare through my reflection, then slowly tilt my head to the glass that's clear and smooth as the surface of water.

Midgets, Jujubes, and Beans

When I was a kid, I heard the rumor that a manager sent a midget to bat in the major leagues. The rumor circulated among the boys in our Little League, but we didn't know if it was true or just some crazy story somebody made up, so the kids on our team usually laughed it off. The only kid who didn't laugh about it was Martin Halsey, who always wore a purple and black checkered shirt, ate Jujubes, and was the smallest player in Little League.

This midget rumor was the kind of story that kids like Martin Halsey thrived on, since he was only four feet five and weighed about eighty pounds. No doubt Martin thought of that midget as someone smaller than he who had actually made it to the majors. Martin believed. But it was also the kind of story that the big guys, the catchers and first basemen, used to scoff at, because in their minds, the only kinds of players who would ever make it were the brawny, powerful guys like themselves.

When we were in sixth grade, I was neither small nor big, but somewhere in the middle. I did often think about growing larger, though, and there were some signs that it might happen. For one thing, I had huge feet for my age and wore size ten shoes. The coach, walking by as I laced my tennis shoes one day, remarked with a grin on his face, "You're going to grow into a big boy some day, Chad. With feet that size, you're going to be big."

"Yeah." I smiled hopefully, wiggling my toes inside my shoes.

Sometime during that summer, my buddy Tommy and I started picking on Martin Halsey. We picked on Martin because he had no friends, because he had a pockmarked face, because he was a weak hitter and a lousy fielder. We picked on him because sometimes, when the baseball came bouncing out to right field—where his team's captain always stuck him—Martin would be peering at the dandelions or chasing butterflies with his mitt. We picked on him because he wore the same short-sleeved purple and black checkered shirt—tucked into his high waist—day after day for an entire year. We picked on him because he always ate Jujubes—those tiny, translucent candy pieces with a weak, sugary taste nobody else liked—and he kept several boxes in his desk at school. When he smiled, you could see the pastel yellows and pinks and greens stuck between his teeth. We picked on him because he spoke in a high voice with a kind of spitty slur, and rolled his eyes as he'd tell everyone the story of the midget in the major leagues for the zillionth time. We started to think Martin was the one who had made up the whole midget thing in the first place. We picked on him because he slicked his hair down and parted it in the middle, though one lock always stayed pasted across his forehead, just above his eyebrow. But more than anything else, we picked on him because he was small, and we were bigger than he was. That was what it came down to, really—we picked on him simply because he was the smallest kid in Little League that summer.

Tommy and I used to think of elaborate ways to taunt Martin. Some days, before the games, we'd pour honey inside the fingers of his baseball glove. We'd find his Jujubes in his duffel bag, dump them in the bushes, replace them with pebbles from the infield, then seal the box shut again. Or we'd pull off his old St. Louis Browns baseball cap and dance across the outfield with it, tossing it back and forth in a game of keepaway. Eventually we'd jump up and hang it on a high nail on a light pole. We'd laugh as Martin stayed on the field for an hour after the game, jumping and jumping for the cap he'd never reach.

Despite the taunting, Martin still hung around us like we were his buddies, and that only made us madder. Earlier that spring, at school, we'd catch him alone after recess, standing by the cloakroom beneath the picture of Jesus wearing a crown of thorns.

"Hey Halsey," we'd hiss, "wanna fight?"

To our amazement, his face always went sort of blank and he said, "Yeah."

We'd tell Martin to meet us by the shed in the alley near the grade school. After school he'd come walking, slump-shouldered, down the alley promptly at three-fifteen, where we'd be waiting, doing wheelies on our bikes. Then, one by one we'd take him on. I might be first, or Tommy might be first, and we'd stand like professional boxers, our fists bobbing, and punch at Martin. It was as though Martin's face was a window we always wanted to throw a rock through. Martin was too weak to defend himself, and the fight usually lasted only a few seconds. It ended when we'd land a few hard punches and Martin fell on the grass and cried. But then he'd have to fight the other guy, who stood waiting, leaning against the splintered shed. So after Martin wiped his face on his sleeve, he'd stand, tuck in his shirttail, and face his next opponent. We never thought of it as unfair that, each time we challenged him, he had to fight *two* fights, not just one. The puzzling part was that he never chickened out and he never said no. I remember thinking once that I wish he'd just say no, and that would be the end of it. But once he agreed, we couldn't back down either, so we'd just have to go through with it. We probably fought Martin half a dozen times during sixth grade, and it always amazed us a little—and made us mad, too—how he took his punishment with dignity, climbing back to his feet and standing there passively, arms dangling at his sides, after we'd land a good one on his cheek and knock him down.

One afternoon, Tommy and I called his house and, when his mother answered, I spoke in a low voice with a strange accent and asked to talk to Martin. I told him I was a baseball scout and he'd been chosen for the All-American Little League Team and that he should meet me at the bus depot at nine o'clock that night. I'd sign him up for the team, I said. I told him to bring his glove and a paper bag with a can of beans inside. I added the beans thing off the top of my head; there was no real reason for it—it just seemed like a funny idea at the time. As I spoke to Martin, it was all Tommy and I could do to keep from bursting into laughter right on the phone. We held the laughter in, doubled over until our stomachs ached. As I hung up, our laughs exploded and ricocheted off the walls as we sprawled on Tommy's bunk beds.

That night, Tommy and I slipped out of our houses and rode our bicycles past the bus depot. There we saw Martin, standing in the parking lot, shivering in his short-sleeved checkered shirt, holding his glove in one hand, a crumpled paper bag in the other.

When I was pitching during Little League, we played Martin's team, and the captain put Martin in as a pinch hitter to bat with the bases loaded and two out. The only way Martin ever got on base was to draw a walk. Martin knew that. I knew that. Everyone on both teams knew that. Occasionally he'd swing weakly at a pitch, moving the bat with only his wrists, but he'd never hit it. I don't recall Martin ever making contact with the ball—not even a foul tip. He just stood at the plate, shivering, standing too straight and flat-footed, one cheek twitching, and prayed for the gift of a walk. That day, our team screamed at him as I pitched: "Hey batter batter batter! Hey batter batter batter, swing!" He took five pitches—three balls and two strikes, and the litany of heckling got even louder and more intense as the kids on the bench started yelling "Hey pitcher pitcher pitcher!" I wound up on the final pitch and threw a fastball down the middle because I knew Martin wouldn't swing. But my aim wasn't true, and the ball rode toward the outside corner of the plate. Martin let it go, then turned and blinked at the umpire behind him, who was our rec director. The ump hesitated a second. The ball had cut the outside corner of the plate and I was already taking a step toward our bench. "Ball four!" the ump called, and my team members howled and threw up their hands in disgust at the same moment that Martin's teammates leaped into the air in a cheer.

I was so angry I kicked up a cloud of dust from the pitcher's mound.

With Martin on first, Tommy held up his big first baseman's mitt. "Pick him, Chad," Tommy said to me between his teeth. "C'mon, buddy. Pick him." Martin took a lead of a few steps and stood there, feet too close together, hands at his sides. My plan was to pick him off for the third out. I went into the stretch, and pretended to check the runner at third. Suddenly I whirled and threw my hardest fastball toward Tommy's mitt. As the ball approached the glove, Martin, on his way back to the bag, stepped in front of its path, and the ball hit him square in the eye. For an instant after the ball struck him, the field went silent. Then a collective groan rose. When Martin fell to the ground with a wail, I was sure his face had cracked like an eggshell.

I stood over Martin, watching his small, scrawny body writhe in pain on the powdery infield dust. With both hands, he clutched his eye, from which ebbed a trickle of blood. I knew the ball had hit him ten times harder than any of the punches we threw at him. I was certain I had blinded him. I remember bending over him as he cried in pain, saying, "You all right, Martin? Sorry. You all right?" I grabbed his arm with my hand and tried to lift him to his feet.

Martin sat up and glared at me, his face streaked with tears and blood. "Get your hands off me!" he shouted, shaking his arm free and climbing to his feet by himself. "You hit me on purpose."

I stood there, stunned. I couldn't say a word to respond to him. Then a feeling of guilt poured over me like cold water, giving me goosebumps. Why *shouldn't* he think I did it on purpose? I thought. After all these years, why would he ever trust me? Our rec director led the weak-legged Martin to his car and drove him to the hospital.

Later that afternoon, I rode my bike to Martin's apartment. He lived in a dingy flat above an old brick downtown store. His mother, a shrill woman with a pointed nose, opened the door just a crack and didn't want to let me in. "*You're* Chad Stevens?" She spoke angrily. She asked me why I was at their door after I'd done so many rotten things to Martin. I turned to leave, and then I heard the high, scratchy sound of Martin's voice behind her, telling her to let me in.

I walked slowly inside and found him sitting in his dim living room, an ice pack pressed to his face. When he looked up at me, I was relieved to see he wasn't blind. We sat on the sagging sofa beneath a framed picture of Jesus. He kept his head tipped back, and I remember his purple, puffed-up eye staring at me distrustfully as I shook his hand and tried to apologize. I talked to him a while as we sat in front of a rickety blond coffee table. I even mentioned the story of the midget coming to bat in the major leagues.

"Probably not true, anyway," Martin said.

Before I left, I pulled a baseball out of my pocket, offered it as a gift, but he said he didn't want it.

A few months later, in junior high school, Martin moved with his mother to another town. For the next two years, there were rumors about him in our school, and kids occasionally laughed and said they heard Martin still wore that same checkered shirt all the way through junior high.

When I was a sophomore in high school, I was standing in the aisle of the theater with Tommy before the start of a movie, and in walked Martin Halsey. He'd come back to town for the weekend. The shadow of whiskers darkened his cheek, and his voice was much lower when he spoke, but he still wore that old, faded St. Louis Browns baseball cap, only the cap looked too small for his head now. He gave me a half-smile, shook my hand.

"Hey Chad," he said. "How's my old pal?"

As I stood there with him in the aisle, I realized he was an inch or two taller than I was, and he looked like he weighed a lot more.

He said he had a girlfriend now, and that he played football, and he might try out for the high school baseball team next spring. He spoke with confidence, his shoulders no longer rounded. Between sentences, he popped some Jujubes into his mouth from a large seventy-five-cent box he bought at the theater candy counter. He said he'd been lifting weights since eighth grade, and I could see his muscles bulge beneath his untucked T-shirt. "You know," he said, "I always used to wish that I could punch you and Tommy out."

His comment put me on edge, and I glanced around for the safety of my friends, who were sitting a few rows down with their feet on the seats, tossing popcorn into the air and catching it in their mouths. I leaned one hand against the slashed red velvet of a theater seat.

"But I was always too small," he continued. "Now that I'm about your size, I probably could." He paused a few seconds in the near dark, letting the words sink in. Then his face widened into a grin. "But don't worry, I'd never do that."

"I've got to go," I said nervously. "Movie's starting."

"Wait a minute," Martin said. "I've just got to ask you one thing."

"What?" I asked.

"The beans," he said.

"Huh?" I replied, puzzled.

"What was the can of beans for?"

All through the movie, as I sat with my buddies, I couldn't help but think about Martin, and what happened to the kid who used to chase butterflies in right field. I kept picturing him, a few years before, standing in the bus depot lot, frail, alone, shivering, holding that paper bag. I kept thinking about how much Tommy and I laughed at him that night as we rode our bikes back home, the silver spokes of our wheels glistening as we pedaled beneath the streetlight. But most of all I remembered the hopeful look on Martin's face as he'd tell the story about the midget who batted in a major league baseball game.

I never saw Martin again after that night in the theater. There were some new rumors about him—that he was popular in his high school, that he made the honor roll, and that he was a star on the baseball team.

A few years later, after high school graduation, I came upon an article in a baseball book. On August 19, 1951, Bill Veeck, owner of the St. Louis Browns baseball team, sent a pinch hitter, a midget named Eddie Gaedel, to the plate. Eddie stood three feet seven inches. The article never stated whether or not the bases were loaded, but I imagined they were. At any rate, Gaedel walked on four pitches—all of them high. It was his only at-bat in the major leagues. I was stunned as I read it; the rumor I'd heard as a kid, the rumor we all assumed was utter crazy nonsense, suddenly became true.

That evening after I read the article, I closed my eyes and pictured the midget, his face small and innocent, like a child's, as he watched the pitches fly above his head. Then I pictured his tiny, puckery face turning into Martin Halsey's face, the same way I'm picturing it now. I see Martin again in Little League, walking on my three-and-two pitch. I see him, taking his lead from first base, standing flat-footed in his purple and black checkered shirt, nodding at me as if he knows what must happen next. I turn and throw hard to first and he centers his face in front of the ball, and I hear the fleshy slap as the ball strikes him. Then I rush over, more sorry than I've ever been, and reach down to help him. This time he doesn't resist as I lift his small body from the ground, and he slowly rises to his feet until he is standing and facing me. It doesn't surprise me that he seems taller than I am. With an expression I can't quite interpret, he just stares into my eyes, looking down at me with that bleeding, black and blue face which suddenly looks so much like mine.

Caught off Base:
Vietnam Baseball

Bob, when you and the rest of the guys set up a little baseball field in the meadow, you laughed your usual high-pitched laugh as you tossed down the sandbag bases. It was 1968, and it could have been a meadow anywhere—in the middle of Wisconsin or somewhere in Oregon or even in rural New Jersey. The only difference was you guys were all dressed in that ugly green: faded green T-shirts with dogtags dangling from chains around your necks, baggy green pants and black boots weighing down your feet. Your faces were smudged, like kids'. You guys called your team the Green Giants. It was a lot of fun for you, setting up that field, deciding on which palm tree was a foul pole, then spray-painting its trunk fluorescent red. The only difference was you guys were in the middle of a war. The rest of us, lucky with the draft, watched on the flat screens of our black-and-white television sets. We couldn't really see the colors on our sets, so we had to imagine them. In 1968, some of us watched the *Game of the Week* on Saturday afternoons, and there were a few good ballplayers and a few good match-ups, but baseball didn't matter all that much during those years. It was just a game.

But it mattered to you, Bob. You talked it up in the mess tent, you spread the word to the guys in the firebase that maybe, one of these mornings, they could get together and play a little

American baseball. "I kid you not," you told everyone, cupping your hand around an imaginary ball. "Think of it. Baseball in the jungle."

For the game, you used a mop handle for a bat and a hard, black rubber ball somebody bought from a toy vendor in Saigon. You couldn't help but giggle as you held the makeshift bat on your shoulder, waiting for the first pitch in the clearing, the morning sun still low behind you. You stood in silhouette and you appeared larger than you actually were, more muscular, ready to hit a long-distance shot, so that some of the guys thought *Ted Williams, Mickey Mantle, Moose Skowron,* and they backed up a step or two.

You could have been standing in a meadow anywhere, flanked by succulent green trees. You could have been standing in the Elysian Fields. The only difference was these trees were jungle trees, broad-leafed, choked with tangled vines. Surrounding them, elephant grass that could slash the skin like a razor.

I remember you from St. Jude's Catholic Grade School, when you organized the games against the seventh graders. The sixth-grade boys would take on the seventh graders in baseball, and though they were bigger than we were, we'd always put up a pretty good fight. We'd use white linoleum squares for bases on the wide asphalt playground, and the nuns, dressed in their pale robes, would sigh and fold their arms beneath the front panels of their habits and watch us. Even the plaster statues, though they didn't have any eyes, watched us from their brick shrines at the corners of the church. We'd play with a rubber ball, which, it seemed, if you hit it between fielders, would roll a thousand miles on that hard asphalt surface. You were tall, and long-legged—you were Bob Crawler, the fastest kid in sixth grade. *Legs,* we called you. I remember how you'd always hit the ball short but very high in the air. Sometimes you'd launch a towering pop-up over the shortstop, and you'd already be rounding second base before the ball would fall from the sky. If one of the seventh-grade kids didn't catch it on a fly, you'd have a sure triple.

After recess, no matter if we lost or not, you'd grin at me with your smudged face, reach out, slap my hand, and say, "Outstanding game, man." After recess, no matter if we lost or not, you'd pass me a few Sugar Babies from behind our raised desktops. You were my good friend, Bob. You were everybody's good friend.

When you set up your makeshift baseball game in 1968, it was easy for us to lean back on our couches and watch you from living rooms in Wisconsin or Oregon or New Jersey. After dinner, on the five-thirty news, it was easy for our town to watch the Green Giants warming up, clowning and tossing a ball back and forth on an evening news feature about Vietnam. It was easy to hear the reporter talk about how the boys always managed to find some recreation over there, and though there was a war going on, how they still had a sense of humor. He spoke close to the microphone, saying we should remember that the boys over there were still just that—American boys. You made the highlight films that night, Bob. You made the national news with your ball game. Your wry, familiar smile—delayed by transmission a couple seconds—stretched all the way home.

It was easy for us to watch. It was easy for us, after the news, to flip the channel to Ed Sullivan or *Gunsmoke* or whatever else happened to be on.

What wasn't so easy was what happened next in Vietnam. We never saw it. But that morning you hit the ball in the air, Bob, as you always did on the grade school playground outside St. Jude's Catholic School. You hit the ball high, and as you raced around the bases, looking up with your smudged face, you heard all the guys on your team screaming for you. A whole country was screaming for you, Bob. As you rounded second, your bouncing dogtags glinting in the sun, the small meadow was hit by incoming rocket fire. With the sudden explosion, you fell. Halfway between bases, your legs just seemed to crumple beneath you, and you fell, and lay motionless. Who knows what went through your mind those last few seconds? Who knows if you felt a lot of pain, or if it was just a bright numbness from the waist down? If it was brightness, then it was a brightness that was not holy: It was just a kind of amazement, it was just a kind of terror.

All you knew was when you reached down for your legs, they were no longer there. Just air and stubble grass in the place where they'd been. You might have mumbled a quick prayer, as we always did in grade school each day before class, early in the morning, the harsh fluorescent lights glistening off the silver crucifix hanging from Sister Agatha's neck. Or maybe you lay there those few seconds, your mind telling you *I'm just on the school playground,* telling you *I just sprained my ankles rounding second—nothing more.* It was just a game. You're in sixth grade, and you're lying there between bases thinking, any second, you'll be tagged out by some seventh-grade kid with a quick glove. But before the kid can reach down to tag you with the ball, the large brass bell on the wall of the school rings. It rings loud every day at the end of recess, chimes out its piercing, high-pitched sound and, according to playground rules passed down from class to class for years, the game's over. The game's over, and you're free, and no one, no one can tag you out.

*   *   *

From our living rooms, before we flipped the channel, we watched the newscast on our small flat screens, and we saw you standing in the low sun in Vietnam, a mop handle on your shoulder, grinning into the camera. And for some reason you looked bigger than you ever looked when we saw you around town, and we leaned forward from our couches and smiled and nodded our heads in relief and thought: *At least he's safe.*

The Call

Mornings are coffee and donuts and waiting at the local café where nobody knows your name, thinks Ronnie Held. Mornings are donuts dry as the infield dirt, and coffee with cumulus clouds rising inside the cup as you pour in thick cream and try not to think of rain. When you're a ballplayer, you try not to think of rain. After his breakfast, Held waits for his check from the waitress, then slowly follows the sidewalk to the motel. Lately his whole life is a narrow path from the motel to the field and back to the motel again. Even his walking is a kind of waiting, and, at the same time, it's a dance, his legs springing him an inch or two toward the sky with each step. He strolls down the tiny windswept main street, toward the motel, his home for the past five months. Strolls past the houses with some of their windows boarded. Past the kids' tricycles tangled on the gravel driveways, past the tiny explosions of dandelions in the patchy yards, past the abandoned baseball bats with their trademarks worn off.

Ronnie steps beneath the overhang above the motel door, glances at the parallel rows of pink and green neon lights above him. At night they buzz like insects, their bright glow filtering through the curtains. He opens the lock with the diamond-shaped plastic keyholder, then pushes the door with one shoulder. He tries not to stare at the phone—the black phone that hasn't rung all season, the phone he sometimes stares at for hours in his dreams, the dumb phone he tries to avoid in his waking. He's waiting for the call. He's heard the voice, rehearsed it in his head dozens of times since he arrived in this tiny minor league town early in March: *Ronnie, you've been called up. Just heard from the majors, and they want you to report in. Better pack your stuff, kid.*

He still feels his numb tongue, which was scalded by the coffee he was too anxious to drink, still tastes the cinnamon donut—so stale he's begun to hate them, yet he keeps eating them morning after morning.

The minor leagues are like that, he thinks. Things have become stale for him, like the listless walk to the ballpark, like sliding on the spikes, like seeing the manager give you that same bored look as he prepares the roster. Like the same graffiti scratched on the back walls of the wooden dugout, the deep letters polished, almost smooth from the shoulders of the players leaning against them day after day. You jog onto the ungroomed field, and you stand in shallow center where a worn spot in the dry grass tells you to stand. Then you wait.

You wait, pitch by pitch, inning by inning, the cloud of dust from the infield rising and blowing out toward you; when the gust reaches you, you have no choice but to close your eyes. You feel the dust coating your throat like sandpaper as you breathe. You play hard, and well, making the catches you need to make, the ball somehow finding your glove. But you're getting older year by year, and the coordination begins to slip from your fingertips and sometimes you make an error on a looping fly ball.

Then you're at bat, and maybe you get some hits. Maybe you take out your anger on that leather sphere and send it flying, flying beyond the wooden scoreboard in left, above the words NORTH JUNCTION painted across the top in dripping whitewashed letters.

Then the game's over, inevitably, just as it began. The

game's over and somebody wins, somebody loses; they hang numbers on the hooks after each inning, and you wonder if it matters. Maybe only the dust, swirling around home plate, matters. Only the dust seems to know where it's going, circling around and around itself lazily, madly.

All Held wants is to be called up by the majors. He doesn't know how many more seasons he'll play, but all he needs is that one call. Every day as he slips on his wrinkled minor league uniform—a little too tight this season—he thinks about the majors. He catches a glimpse of himself in the big locker room mirror—Ronnie Held, an unknown minor leaguer in a tiny Midwest town in the middle of nowhere. He doesn't fit, doesn't fit in either world right now.

Held tosses his duffel bag on the bed, flips on the black-and-white TV that makes the whole room look fuzzy.

He steps to the calendar tacked to the dark paneled wall, gazes absently at the girl in a two-piece swimming suit standing beside a new 1964 Chevy, its paint glowing candy-apple red, then marks an X on the date July 21. The summer's moving by quickly, he thinks, and the calendar's filled with X's—May, June, and now July. Each X is a small crossroad: Another day's passed.

At that moment the telephone—a phone that's been still for weeks—suddenly rings. He leaps toward it and slaps the receiver to his ear.

"Yes?"

But the line clicks dead, a missed connection. Only the scratchy buzz of the dial tone pours out.

Held strolls down the street to the laundromat; in the town of North Junction, it's a combination bowling alley and laundromat. He's stuffed a pillow case with his socks and jerseys. *You're responsible for your own laundry, boys,* the coach told them. *Keep your uniforms like new,* he always repeated—*you look like a ballplayer and you'll feel like a ballplayer, and if you feel like a ballplayer, then you'll play like a ballplayer.* The coach always has such pat sayings, thinks Held, as if believing them could actually make you a success. After he yanks open the big glass doors and dumps his clothes into a Maytag, he notices a woman sitting at the far end of the room reading a movie magazine. She looks up for a moment, seems to smile, then bows her head to the magazine again.

Out of the corner of his eye he sees her watching him as he pulls out the washed laundry. He stares at the wet socks in his hand, sees the brown smiles of dust where the rims of his shoes meet his ankles. The socks never come clean, he thinks. It's the dust, the dust in the batter's box that's ground to a powder by the thousands of cleated shoes. He piles the wet clothes into his arms, carries them up the aisle and tosses them into a dryer. As he's digging into his pocket for a coin, he notices someone at his elbow. It's the woman: her long, light hair tied back. She's not young, exactly, but not old either. She's slim, dressed in blue jeans, and wears a washed-out flowered blouse, still clean and pretty in its own way. She holds up a sock with her long, slender hand.

"You dropped something," she says.

"Oh" is all Held can blurt. He reaches for the sock.

She pulls the sock back slightly. "You could say thank you."

"Yeah, yeah. Thanks." Held's face brightens, and he lowers his eyes. With his hair matted from sweat, his face tanned only on the bottom half, he wishes he was still wearing his ball cap. He turns and throws the sock into the dryer.

She begins a sentence, though he still has his back turned. "Next time . . ." she says.

He pivots, and when he does, he finds himself close to her face.

"Next time," she repeats, half of her mouth curling into a smile, "try using some bleach."

"Oh." He rubs his sunburned neck. "Yeah. Bleach." He gazes into her face a moment. It's white and milky.

"I've never seen you around town," she says.

"I'm a ballplayer," he mumbles.

"Oh. One of those." Her words sink a little into her throat.

"What's that supposed to mean?" He wrinkles his forehead.

"Well . . ." She pauses, straightens the pale collar on her blouse. "It's just that the baseball players never seem to stay long in this town."

He glances into the dryer, her white clothes fluttering around and around. "How about you?" he asks. "What do you do?"

"I give voice lessons."

"Voice?" Held squints one eye. "What's that?"

"You know, singing." She leans her hip against the warm oval window of a dryer.

"Oh. You're a singer, then?"

"No, not really," she says modestly, lowering her gaze a moment. "I just teach people to sing." She tucks one knee under and turns herself toward him. "Do you know anything about singing?"

"No," he says, shaking his head. "Afraid I don't. I'm just a ballplayer."

"You've got a nice-sounding voice."

"I do?"

"You do," she says, and smiles at him.

Held can feel his face tingle as it turns red again, and he's not sure how to respond. Finally he comes up with something. "You ever get over to any of the games?" He raises his voice above the whirr of a nearby machine that's gone into its spin cycle.

"No, not lately."

"What do you mean, not lately?"

"Well . . ." Her eyes seem to turn sad a few seconds, and then her expression hardens. "I used to go to a few games. But that was a long time ago."

"So," he says, nodding at the movie magazine in her hand, "so you go to movies then?"

"Not since the theater closed," she says.

"Oh," he stammers. "Yeah. Well maybe you should go sometime."

"Go to the movies?"

"No, I mean to a game."

There's no response in her face. With a sound like a sigh, her dryer stops running, and she leans over and opens the door. She pulls a corner of a sheet out and tests it gingerly with her fingertips. She pushes it back in, and with one graceful motion she pulls a dime from her front jeans pocket, clicks it into the slot and the clothes tumble again. "Just in case I do," she finally says, "tell me. What number are you?"

By the time Held's load is dry, the woman is gone. She walked out with a wicker basket full of neatly folded white sheets, her magazine balanced on top of the stack. She smiled at him briefly as she backed through the swinging doors. Held tossed a smile back to her and then shrugged at no one after she left. He was never much with women, never knew quite how to react. He was much more at ease on the ball field, standing on the solid ground of center field.

As he steps out the door of the laundromat, his pillow-case stuffed with clean clothes, he notices that the outside ledge of the front window is covered with June bugs. They're drawn toward the fluorescent lights of the big rectangular picture window. Dazed June bugs: bunched in the corners and on the wooden windowsill, drawn to the window bright as a movie screen, drawn to the white whirring machines and the sheets spinning around and around. The insects thump against the glass, and some of them fall to the sidewalk. On their backs, they move their legs in the air, doing a kind of slow-motion dance. He tries to avoid them as he steps, but the bugs crackle beneath his shoes.

Held drops off his laundry at the motel, and though it's nearly sunset, he feels some sudden energy, so he picks up his baseball bat and duffel bag, jogs down to the empty field to hit a few fly balls toward the black, numberless scoreboard. All of his hits fall short, and in the dusk he has trouble finding some of them, their blond skins blending with the dry bleached outfield grass. She was kind of pretty, he thinks. And she smiled at him. Was she interested? No, he thinks. Then he says it aloud to himself. "No." He reads the team name above the splintering scoreboard. SILVERSTARS. He ponders the name a moment, then asks himself: Who ever heard of the North Junction Silverstars? His teammates brag in the dugout and they keep their distance. They brag, but no one's ever heard of this little minor league team. No. The outfields are all weeds.

Before he leaves, he steps close to the backstop, tosses a ball into the air, and hits it hard into the wires. It clinks against the aluminum. He picks the ball up, hits it again. Hits it again and again until, in the darkness of early evening, the fence nearly sings.

He lies on the motel's scratchy sheets, slipping gradually toward grainy sleep. The ring startles him, and he leaps to the small end table where the phone sits. He stares at it, and it rings again. He sees the tiny red light pulsing on top of the phone.

He picks it up. "Yeah?" he says.

"Hello," a voice says on the other end of the line. "Who is this?"

"Who's this?"

"Oh, I'm sorry. Wrong number, I guess," the voice says.

The voice is liquid, smooth, syrupy. A woman's voice, its edges soft.

"What number you trying to reach?"

"I'm . . ." the voice hesitates. "I'm not sure. . . ." Then the connection breaks and the dial tone buzzes in Held's ear, buzzes inside his head all night long as he sleeps.

The next afternoon at the game, he comes to the plate in the ninth. So far in this game, he's o for 4, and he made an error in center when an easy looping fly ball bounced off the heel of his glove. The team's behind by two runs, and runners wait at second and third. Held can sense his manager's eyes on him; the stare weighs down his wrists as though rocks were tied to them. On a three-and-two pitch Held swings for the scoreboard and the bat breaks; the ball flies weakly and the left fielder takes a few steps forward, then gloves it for the final out of the game.

The following day, in the laundromat, she glides up to him, hands behind her back, then holds up a sock and laughs.

"You dropped another one," she says. "Do you make a habit of this?"

"Aw jeez," he says, blushing, shaking his head.

"It's okay to drop one," she says, noticing his embarrassment. "Don't worry about it."

His mind flashes back to yesterday's game. Had she seen him drop that ball? he wonders. He grabs the sock from her. It looks pure and white.

"My name's Clare, by the way," she says. There's a kind of light beneath her skin as she says her name. She holds out her hand.

"Oh. Yeah," he says, almost stuttering. "Held. Ronnie Held. Center fielder."

She laughs lightly at his response as he takes her hand in his. "Center fielder?"

"Yeah," he says, puzzled. "Why'd you laugh?"

"Oh, just the *way* you said it. Like it was your official title or something. Like you should wear it on a tag on your lapel."

He shrugs. "It's what I do."

As they sit down on the card-table chairs next to the white Formica table while their laundry dries, he notices a thin booklet in her lap.

"What's that you're reading?" he asks.

"Just a music score." She flips through the pages with her thin fingers. "It's an opera. You know anything about opera?"

"You kidding?" He chuckles.

"I love operas." She glances down at the score, runs her fingers along the staples in its spine. "They have such feeling."

"Yeah," he says. His voice sounds flat in his ears, and he doesn't mean it to sound that way.

"The music really affects me. The way it rises and falls." She takes a deep breath, then stares at the ceiling. "Operas take me places I've never been." She turns her head toward Held. "I've lived here all my life, you know."

"Here? In North Junction?" He shakes his head side to side. "You're lucky to survive."

"Yes," she exhales, "I am."

She leans toward him a few seconds, her elbows like pale porcelain on the Formica. Then she stands up and maneuvers through the overweight housewives, dressed in pants and faded floral blouses, their hair twisted in pin curlers, who bend over cracked plastic laundry baskets. She stops at the soda machine, drops a quarter into the slot. She glides back to the chair, takes a sip of her Sunkist, and sighs. "Did it ever occur to you how much time people waste here?" she says.

"Huh?"

"People wash and dry these clothes just to wear them again. Then they come back in and wash them all over again."

"So?"

She gazes at him intently. "Some people do things over and over in life and they never think to stop or change a little. They never *think* about being spontaneous. Do you know what I mean?"

He knew she wasn't talking about laundry now. He knew it was about something else, but he couldn't quite follow the direction.

"Yeah, I s'pose" was all he could muster.

* * *

Standing in the outfield during the game, Held thinks about Clare. He thinks about what she said. He thinks about how minor league ballplayers never last long in North Junction. It's late August, the final stretch of the '64 season already, and he'll be leaving for his home in Oklahoma in a couple of weeks. The team's in last place, and the manager mutters and players clench their teeth through loss after loss. Some of his teammates won't be back next spring. If they don't get called up—and no one has yet—they drop out after a season or two; some don't get their contracts renewed, some get injured, and some, nearing thirty, realize they're just too worn and tired to ever make it. Last week, a teammate—a fellow outfielder—was taken off the roster because his eyes got too bad; he tried glasses and contacts, but nothing helped. Held knows that losing the eyesight is the outfielder's biggest fear. When the eyesight begins to go, it gets harder and harder to pick up the ball as it rises off the bat. Held sometimes imagines how it might look from the outfield: First the bat whips around, and you hear the sound of an echoing crack, then the infielders turn toward your field and tilt their heads back, but you see nothing, nothing. You scour the sky, but all you see is blue, endless blue; you keep squinting for that white thumbtack that seems stuck up there for good. You hold your arms out to your sides helplessly as your infielders point and shout, "There! There!" When the fly ball lands twenty feet from you, it lands with a thud you keep hearing all night in your sleep.

* * *

Held wakes in the middle of the night to the thud. He looks on the floor and sees a dull shine from the black phone. Bumped it off the night stand, he thinks.

He picks up the phone, steadying the receiver on its cradle. At just that moment, the phone rings. Or at least he thinks it rings—it's just a short, subtle *ting* as if it were the very end of a ring. Nothing, he thinks—the drop messed up the wiring.

But he pulls the receiver from the phone anyway and draws it slowly to his ear.

"Yes?" he says, thinking, for an instant, that it could be the coach, who might bark: *Pack your stuff, kid. They've called you up.*

Instead, there's no sound on the other end of the line—no dial tone, no operator.

Another wrong number, he thinks.

Then he hears something through the black wires—a soft breathing, followed by a sound that's melodic and flowing. He sits up silently, listening. It's a woman's voice, fresh and pure and beautiful, gliding through the thin black wires of the telephone, and she's singing to him.

THREE

Between Innings:
Kirby Puckett's
Legs and
Other Visions

Kirby Puckett's Legs:
A Symphony in Nine Innings

1

At night, in the middle of the long cold sigh of winter, the sky covered by a tarpaulin, small boys in Minnesota sleep in baseball jerseys and dream of Kirby Puckett's legs. They see them, moving like pistons, pumping Kirby around first toward second as his hit careens off the outfield wall. The score's tied in the ninth, and for a moment it looks like Kirby's running in place.

2

But no. He's merely accelerating. Kirby Puckett's legs: thumping turkey drumsticks, adrenalized heartbeats.

3

All winter, in bedrooms across Minnesota, some husbands and wives sleep with a baseball in their bed. He dreams of making that amazing diving catch he missed once in Little League. She dreams of her grass-stained husband jogging toward her, staring into her eyes, brushing the hair from her face with his soft, gloved hand.

4

Now husbands and wives wake to the sound of their small son's dream, wake to the staccato of Kirby rounding second, the music of fans screaming.

5

On defense, it's Kirby on the blinding green of center field. Quick hop-steps to get under the fly ball, baby-steps to find the exact spot where the pinhead will drop from the folds of the curved white sky. On the drives to deep center, Kirby waits casually at the fence as though he's standing at a bus stop. Suddenly he leaps. When he returns to earth, he brings back smiling white leather in the web of his glove.

6

Kirby swings a wide crescendo around third and the fans rise from the dead and stand, all fifty-five thousand of them stand on their one hundred ten thousand weak, spindly legs. They lift their voices in unison: "Home, Kirby! Home!"

7

He churns toward the plate, a drumroll. Here comes the throw from left. Here comes Kirby. He slides with a gasp.

8

After the play, Kirby climbs to his feet, then shrinks smaller and smaller, shrinks until he's a boy again. He's standing in a sandlot, grinning, waiting for the pitch, knowing he's about to hit the first home run of his life.

9

In the Metrodome, after the win, we smile along with him, and for a moment, we dream.

For a moment our lives are perfect as Kirby Puckett's legs.

The Man Who
Rescued Baseballs

If you've ever walked through the long grass at the edge of a ball field, stepped on what you thought was a small mound of dirt pushed up by a mole, and looked down to see a baseball, then you'd know what he feels. He is the finder of lost baseballs.

He is the man who walks the perimeter of every ball field in town. He is the man who combs the field with his palm, hearing an odd litany running through his head: *Give me your poor, your tired, your homeless. Your huddled masses yearning to be free.* The best way to find them, he'll tell you, is by bending to one knee, then looking at the field from different angles, your head tilted left or right. The best way to find them is by walking in the scrub brush behind the field where nobody walks, where floating spiderwebs sometimes cling delicately to your face, or small, sharp branches lash across your cheeks.

He finds the baseballs in dried weeds, yellowing to camouflage themselves. He finds them abused and burrowed into mud. Sometimes he finds them white and almost new, but usually he finds them weathered, grayed, like the tops of small skulls half-submerged in the soil. When he picks them up in spring, he sees the effects of sitting motionless through the ice and cold of a long winter—they're heavy with water, and sometimes their seams are torn, exposing the frantic windings of string within.

His friends say he's strange—strange for keeping the found baseballs loose in the back window of his old car, where they roll and thump at every turn. He's strange for covering the floor of his garage with them instead of parking his car there. Once his wife, searching for a yard rake, stepped on a ball and twisted an ankle. He's strange for keeping them in a kitchen cabinet among the cans of tomato puree and the marshmallow cream.

He's kind to each new find as he cleans it with a soft towel. He learns every stitch, learns to recognize the faces of his adopted children. When he jogs to a field to hit a few fly balls, he pulls them out of the duffel bag and greets each one. He has their family backgrounds down pat, knows which balls he found in Fargo or Sioux City, Baraboo, Wisconsin, or Ball Club, Minnesota. He might hold a recent find close to his lips and tell it, "You're from the generation of Spaldings." Or: "You're a Rawlings." Or: "Don't forget that you belong to a family of Diamonds."

Then there are others with the mixed or unknown heritage—those worn, tired baseballs that have been hit so many times they'd never be identified by their family names. They're often dark brown, not much different from the smooth round stones that have pushed their way up for a breath of air in the spring. It's these baseballs he loves the best: They're the experienced and wise ones, they're the survivors. Before they were lost, they might have scraped against the clouds with their bellies, or bounced on asphalt that left bruised scuff marks; they might have rolled all the way across America.

He often thinks of the careless ballplayers who leave baseballs on a field. He often thinks of those in a hurry, those impatient people with no time or care, those who would rush to their sleek cars and leave the small things behind to die and rot. He dislikes those types, dislikes their indifference toward everything that matters. He's not in a hurry. He could spend all afternoon searching the edges of a field just to rescue a single ball.

Sometimes he begins to think that he really doesn't find the baseballs, it's the baseballs that find *him*. They search him out, lift themselves toward him when they see his long legs come swinging through the spokes of grass. *You,* they seem to be whispering in their leather silence. *You.*

"Enough baseballs," his wife says. "Enough enough enough. What will you ever do with that many?"

He doesn't answer her question. He loves her for tolerating him, for tolerating his extended family that bursts from the closet like popcorn overflowing a kettle.

"Really," she continues. "What could you possibly do with all those?"

"A player can never have enough baseballs," he finally replies. "You know how easily they can get lost."

"Yes," she replies, "but it's *everyone else* that loses them. You've never lost one, have you?"

He takes a deep breath. "Once," he replies, a note of regret sounding in his voice. "Once, last year."

One afternoon a few weeks later, when the game is over and the players and fans are gone, he walks into the brush and discovers a ball. He studies it, turning it over and over in his hand like a blind man trying to recognize a face. Yes, he's certain. It's his own baseball. It's the same ball he lost here last year.

That night he dreams his recurring dream: He's leaning over and picking up an old baseball from the grass. Beneath that is another baseball, beneath that, another. The last baseball he finds is so glossy and new that he can see his own face reflected in it, and it's the face of a child. When he wakes, he walks from his bed, lifts his baseballs one by one from the shelf and gazes at them in the moonlight. After all these years, the baseballs seem to think nothing of his kindness. They just sit there—silent, unmoving in his broad palm. But he knows they care. Their red stitches never stop grinning at him.

Before he falls back asleep, the thought occurs to him that his baseballs will probably outlive him. When he's gone, someone might open his closet door and they'll all come spilling out, thudding dully to the floor in a pyramid of grief. Perhaps his young son will lift them tenderly from the floor and place them back in the closet. Perhaps his son will be a finder of lost baseballs.

Freight Trains, Flights of Geese, Shoes, and Homers: The Whole Truth About the Journey of an American Baseball

For my baseball buddies:
Dale, Jim, Mick, and Bill

Like all ballplayers, I have lots of stories to tell, stories taken from the best ash trees on the mountainside, stories cut in long rectangles and dried just the right number of days. Then they're lathed, hewn, shaped to perfection, and covered with the clearest finish. You can believe what you want to believe, but what I'm about to tell you is all true. I swear with my hand on a stack of Louisville Sluggers.

First, let me clear up a few misconceptions about the home run. The history books tell us that Mickey Mantle's six-hundred-foot home run at Yankee Stadium is the longest homer on record. But in the 1920s, when Babe Ruth played a major league exhibition game at Rickwood Field in Birmingham, Alabama, he hit a home run that cleared the fence and landed on a moving freight train. The train did not stop until it reached Nashville, Tennessee, some two hundred miles away.

Sometimes I picture the kids playing around the freight cars at a train yard in Nashville back in the twenties. One of them spots a baseball in the corner of a boxcar, picks it up, and says to the other kids, "Hey, maybe this was hit by Babe Ruth!"

"Sure," a kid says, laughing at him. "I'm sure."

Last year I was playing baseball with some friends, and somebody hit a high pop foul behind home plate. The ball hovered in the air a few seconds, then finally, when it decided to come down, it landed in someone's empty tennis shoe near the backstop.

We walked over and marveled at the baseball, which was stuck tightly in the opening of the shoe. "What are the chances?" we wondered aloud. The guy who owned the shoe vowed that he'd save that shoe exactly as it was, that he'd never take the ball out, that, if he had to, he'd walk the rest of his life with one shoe.

Afterward, in a bar, we drank a few beers. The shoe with the ball stuck in it rested in the middle of our table, a centerpiece surrounded by tall glasses of beer. As we shook our heads in wonder, we talked about it: Maybe that baseball wanted to go for a long walk on foot, we said. A vagabond baseball, someone joked. We all chuckled and nodded in agreement.

Once, just outside Minneapolis, I was hitting baseballs on a field that bordered a railroad track. After a few minutes, I heard the sound of an approaching freight train. The whole field shook beneath my tennis shoes as the train thundered closer. I looked at the train, then down at the baseball in my hand, and, impulsively, took a swing and hit the baseball. The ball flew toward the open boxcars of the train that blinked past. As it dropped behind a small tree, I couldn't tell if the ball fell just short of the train, just beyond it, or if it actually landed on the train. All I know is that I searched for a half hour through the tangled weeds that bordered the track, but I never found that baseball.

I love the sound of a distant train whistle. I love the sound of a high, distant flock of geese as they migrate south in October. I love the soft hissing sound an approaching baseball makes as it parts the still, silent air around it.

Some people think that Babe Ruth's freight-train home run was the longest home run of all. But that's not true. A friend of mine has a baseball that traveled farther. He attached a tag to a baseball, hit it to a friend of his—a postman standing in the door of a jet—and the ball was sent, air mail, from New York to Los Angeles.

I don't understand why I love a brand new baseball so much. It could be that it's unsoiled as the soul before original sin. It could be that it's untainted as our planet before so many humans took over and began to scuff it.

My young son was walking along a freight yard in St. Cloud, Minnesota, on his way to school when he spotted something sitting in the bright open doorway of a parked boxcar. It was a baseball.

He brought it home and showed it to me. "Who do you think hit it?" he asked.

Without hesitation, I answered, "Babe Ruth."

* * *

In a Salvation Army store near Nashville, Tennessee, I noticed the strangest thing. It was a pair of tennis shoes for sale. Stuck inside the opening of one of the shoes was an old baseball. A note was pinned to the shoelaces. It read: THE BASEBALL COMES WITH THESE SHOES.

A famous major leaguer—was it Ruth or Mantle?—had recurring dreams during the offseason. Whenever it was snowing hard outside, he dreamed of standing on the field on the last day of the season and hitting a high fly ball that landed on the back of a flying goose. The ball balanced there as the bird migrated south beneath the full moon.

The longest hit ever recorded took place on the moon and was witnessed by the astronauts of Apollo 11. In a little-publicized event in 1969, Neil Armstrong smuggled a baseball bat under the seat of the *Eagle* landing module and pulled a Spalding baseball from inside his space suit. With the other astronauts watching, he faced the west, ceremoniously tossed the ball into the air, hit it high, and watched it fly hundreds of yards until it disappeared from view.

The next morning, as the astronauts stepped from the lunar module, one of them sighted a round object traveling toward them from the east. At first they thought it was a satellite of some kind, perhaps a lost Russian Sputnik. But it was the baseball, a tiny moon orbiting the larger moon. It confused Mission Control in Houston when they heard a voice say triumphantly, *One small hit for man, one giant homer for mankind.*

* * *

Amazing as they might seem, none of these match the most memorable home run. The greatest home run of all took place after a small boy, playing ball with his dad, was hit in the face by a vicious hop from a bounding grounder. The father rushed over to the boy, who lay crying in the grass. The father dabbed the boy's cheeks with his shirttail, then lifted the boy and cradled him in his arms as he jogged the two blocks back to their house.

If you want to understand the flight of dreams, just talk to old ballplayers in a bar for a while. They'll lift their foamy beer to their lips and exhale story after story. They'll tell you it was last of the ninth, two outs, the crowd on their feet. Then, before they limp out of the bar, the past like a bandage taped gently around one knee, the old ballplayers might stand up in the smoky air, their bodies widened and flabby, squeeze an invisible bat with their fists and show you, in slow motion, the swing that hit the ball out of the park in some league championship a few hazy decades ago.

Baseball stories always get longer and better if they're simmered a few years. They get longer and better if their thirst is quenched by a couple of beers.

Most of what we remember really happened, and a little is invented. Baseball is a lot like that; it begins with real, natural things: a simple stick carved from a hardwood tree, a horse-hide ball white as the full moon on a clear night, a glove made from cow leather. It begins wherever there's a stretch of open grass, an empty city street, a tarred alley. From there, you play the game, and you dream it. No matter how strong or what size you are, all you really need to do is catch a ball, or meet the ball with a bat, and be able to tell a good story afterward.

Perhaps that's it. When it comes down to it, all good baseball players are probably a combination of skilled athletes and deft storytellers. I'm lucky enough to have you reading this story. Maybe right now you're cradling it in your hands, like a newfound baseball in some freight yard, and nodding at it, believing it's all true.

Note Left in the House
for the Widows of the
Over-Thirty Baseball Players

For Christine

For you, who wake at seven-thirty some mornings and find me gone, my duffel bag missing from the closet, a note scrawled on a smudged scorecard on the clean couch, my spilled flakes of Wheaties cemented to the kitchen table like some strange hieroglyphs . . .

For you, who must endure the creaking of my aching muscles as I sleep, the odors of torn college T-shirts, of muddied spikes that curl into themselves in corners, of musty, waterlogged memories that roll across the floor each evening . . .

For you, who never question the logic of my lopsided brain, of broken and rebroken bats healed again and again by glue, wood screws, miles of masking tape, and hope . . .

For you, who, when I lean toward the doorway, glove in hand, asking if it's okay to play some ball, shape your smooth pink lips around the word *Go* . . .

This note is for you.

* * *

Forgive me, your husband, lost somewhere in the bleachers thirty years deep, searching for that one child who looks like me.

This note is for you. Listen to the most honest thing I could say, the resonant sound of my best hit: *I love you.*

I want you always to remember it's a kind of love that makes me leave to play this game each day, that makes me run those bases under a huge, indifferent sky.

And it's a kind of love that pulls me back to the house hours later, winded but a little younger each time, to stand as close to you as humanly possible, to gaze into the clear roundness of your eyes that don't care if I've won or lost.

A Song for
Hank Aaron's Swing

Your swing was so smooth, it could have been a paint-
brush, sweeping broad strokes on the horizon. In '74, you
stood in your tall, relaxed stance, poised on the edge of
Ruth's home run record. You watched the ball roll from the
pitcher's fingers, saw it rotate in the air, and waited.

As a kid, you learned your quick, last-instant swing with
a broomstick, swiping at curving bottle caps pitched to you
by your brother. Batting cross-handed, you were the beauty
of opposites, your thin arms coiled with power. You always
let your silence speak for you.

Once, in Milwaukee County Stadium, I watched you hit
what seemed to be an infield pop-up down the third-base line.
The ball climbed the air and kept climbing, and didn't stop
until, far beyond the outfield fence, it poked a hole through
the glass floor of heaven.

For years since that game, I've replayed that hit in my
mind: That homer was you, Henry, rising so modestly, pushing your shoulders against the heavy sky that tried to hold
you down.

When you were just one swing away from the Babe's record, some idiot fans, seeing only black and white, sent you
death threats.

But you knew a baseball must be set free. So you swung like you always did, and hit the ball squarely, in the place where the whorls in the wood grain kiss leather goodbye. The ball rose for two decades, high above the shacks of Mobile, high above the Negro leagues, the restaurants where they'd break your team's plates after you ate dinner, high above the bigots who walked off the field the moment a black man walked onto it, and high enough to clear that wall called America.

When the ball landed in our backyards on a spring afternoon, our small sons and daughters ran over and picked it up. Not knowing it was from you, Hank, they giggled and began a game of catch, tossing the ball back and forth through the fragrant, colorless air.

Wintering the Season

After the last game of the World Series, sudden cold winds from Canada cross the border and force the grass blades to bow their heads. Walking across a field, he's pushed off balance. Back at home, before he places it on the basement shelf, he centers a ball in his glove's pocket, then stretches a rubber band tightly around it as if to hold the glove still, to keep it from trying to slide back onto his hand.

The days shorten, and he wakes to mornings dark as small closets. Then, one afternoon, the sky begins to snow. He stares out his window, picturing, at the nearby baseball field, the chalk lines icing over, the innocent face of the field suddenly turning pale.

This is the season without baseball; there is no longer season. The pages of the calendar thicken and turn to stone. Spring seems too far away—it's like looking for a pinhole in the sky above the horizon. He's recorded a few of the last big-league ball games on videotape, but it's not the same to watch them when he already knows the scores, when the warm temperatures appear on the screen and he's caught the center of winter, the twenty-below-zero air sharpening its icy teeth on the window glass.

Oh, he thinks, *if only nothing would change, our lives would be right. We'd still live in Eden. Each blade of grass would be a bridge to eternity. The word* love *could be whispered once and it would echo forever.*

But he knows better. He is wintering in America, wintering the television set with its news of murders, of wars, of fists lashing out quickly as cars sliding into the ditches during snowstorms. He is wintering, and somehow his heart feels flat and white like the unplayable fields that surround his small house.

In January, as he drives home from work, the car cutting through ribbons of drifting snow that tangle on the highway, he catches himself daydreaming about spring training. He opens his eyes to a place where everything's green and the air smells like moist earth. He's walking in a short-sleeved shirt across a field surrounded by gardens, a place where the lush vegetation drapes over itself as if to get closer to the sun, where flowers unclench their fingers on vines just beyond the outfield fences. It's a place where the sand around home plate is soft as a beach. He's always thinking ahead these months. If baseball taught him one thing, it taught him this: There's always another game, another inning, *another chance.*

At home, he thinks about the time he and his best buddy played baseball on a field coated with ice. They were in ninth grade, and it was the middle of winter, and they didn't know any better. There was no traction when they ran for the ball with their tennis shoes, but when they took a diving slide and caught one, their dive never seemed to end. Back at the house, they stood in front of the dining room mirror. They laughed and agreed they looked like madmen: the leather of their damp baseball gloves blackened, their clothes torn, their hair matted, sopped with sweat and melted ice. They were only fourteen then, he muses; their limber legs could have jogged through three feet of snow in Siberia; they could have set up a baseball diamond on the back of a glacier.

The next morning, he wakes and realizes everything's different now: His legs step tentatively on the ice-covered ground as if it might crack and he'd fall through to the center of the earth. And when he clears the snow from the sidewalk, his muscles ache for days.

As he puts away his shovel in the garage, he notices, forgotten in the corner, a lone baseball bat. The snow that blew through a crevice in the concrete swirls into a small drift around its barrel. He picks the bat up to carry it to the basement. The wood is cold; it numbs his fingers even through his insulated gloves. He pauses in the driveway where the sun strikes the side of a snowbank. He reaches down, notices that the snow is sticky, and packs a handful of it into a ball. Then he lobs it into the air, swings the bat, and hits it. The snowball bursts with a muffled explosion. He packs another snowball, solid and lopsided, hits it. Then another. He stands there in the middle of winter in the middle of his driveway, hitting snowballs with a baseball bat. When cars drive past, people point at him from the side windows, and he knows he must look like a madman, but after each swing he closes his eyes, imagines the snowballs flying in the air over the swaying green of a palm tree.

The hits feel great on the sweet spot of the bat, though, as each snowball breaks, bits of ice sting his face.

The Glove Lacers

Most often they're overweight, and they wear small, smudged glasses to peer at the strands of leather. They sit on stools beneath harsh, narrow lights, sliding leather back and forth, intertwining it for miles, it seems, through thumb and fingers and webs. They could be in love with this job, or they could hate it, the way they stare for so long at the motionless gloves in front of them on their workbench. But the fact is that they do it simply because someone must pull out the weak, frayed, and broken laces and replace them with the strong.

Their job keeps them from getting lost. They could be spelunkers, explorers finding their way through an endless labyrinth of narrow tunnels. They could be patient teachers, lighting up the tiny synapses of a child's brain, coaxing a slow girl to speak her first word. They could be deliberate scientists, threading their way through the distant galaxies, through equations of space and time and relativity.

But most often, though they rarely say a word, the glove lacers are simply communicators. They're like the telephone operator who connects the call through the maze to the right wires. They connect the glove to itself, which in turn connects to the hand of the player, which in turn connects to the ball.

If you ask him, one man will tell you, shyly, that he is a

glove lacer because his father was a glove lacer. He might tell you he used to play ball once. He seems to be the furthest thing from a baseball player—wearing a brown leather apron on his paunchy body, he appears more like a medieval monk with his ring of balding hair and his scraggly beard. He claims there are at least sixty different patterns in glove lacing, some curving and twisting this way, some crisscrossing that way, and he swears he knows them all. The neighborhood kids crowd around his basement workbench to watch him lace gloves. He shows them the process, his elbows constantly swinging. Before they leave, he gives each of them a short strand of leather and a chocolate from the Russell Stover box on the shelf.

He'll tell you that, when he was a kid back in the fifties, he helped his dad lace the gloves of some of the greats. He pulled their fingers taut, gave their webs the strength they needed to bring a baseball—slicing the infield air at 120 miles an hour— to a stop. He'll tell you that if the laces didn't hold, the ball might tear through the web, trickle into the outfield for a hit. If the laces didn't hold, a baseball glove would be nothing more than a shapeless piece of leather.

There's no fame for the glove lacers, no fortune; no one calls them heroes. When people see a catch, they never think about the glove lacers. The glove lacers know one rule, and they accept it: Once they've taught a glove everything they know about laces, they have to let it go. They let it go. And when the crowd stands and cheers a dazzling backhand at third, the glove lacers sit in the top rows of the stadium, watching, their pudgy fingers laced together in front of their stomachs as they nod and smile.

The Heaven of Baseball

(For Nathan, age seven, who asked: "What
if a game was tied forever?")

If they made leaping catches at the fence, then they leap
again and again, snagging the ball each time in the tips of
their gloves. If they hit grand slams, then the bases are always
loaded when they step to the plate, each pitch a high fastball
they could fall in love with. If they pitched a no-hitter, their
fastballs are blurs in high-speed photographs, their curves
sliver the plate's corners like the edges of razor blades. If they
were umpires, all close calls are fair, and no one, no one
argues.

The players shrug at one another, amazed: Bruises on their
thighs fade and disappear. The splintered bats they broke last
night have healed themselves, the grains fusing together.

In the bleachers, the fans scream in ecstasy with voices that
never get hoarse. A crippled child stands, walks toward the
railing for autographs.

After days, players in the on-deck circle gaze into the shiny
surface of batting helmets, notice their faces still don't need
a shave. Their skin glows without wrinkles, like in their first
Little League snapshot taken in the backyard by their fathers
who never died, who still sit proudly behind home plate,
cheering.

The teams could play another month, a decade, a century
without rain or winter or hunger. Between each inning the

players jog toward the dugout, glance at the endless lines of zeros on the scoreboard, then nod and grin at their opponents.

Finally they understand that nobody wins this one, and nobody loses. The whole world is smooth and flawless as a new baseball.

FOUR

Leaning Toward the Dugout

In the Middle of a Pitch

He wakes before his alarm to the faraway song of an umpire calling a third strike. Standing in front of the bathroom mirror, he leans forward, narrowing his eyes at himself as if he were peering at the catcher for his sign. Then he stretches, his hands high, almost touches the plaster ceiling where the spiderweb cracks seem to lengthen a little each week. When he brings his right arm down in an imaginary pitch, a strike, he feels the old aching. Staring at the arm in the mirror, he wonders how the flesh got so flabby. *It didn't look that way yesterday, did it?* he thinks. Yesterday the tendons were taut and ready like some finely tuned musical instrument; yesterday he was sure he could hear every muscle humming.

Everything happens so fast, he thinks, *everything happens in a day.* One day he's Dusty Sikarsky, starting pitcher for a major league team. The next day he's Dusty Sikarsky, used car salesman, tossing curves at the off-balance customers. As he dresses for work, his mind spans twenty years to the baseball days. He thinks about how you work your way up through the leagues: First it's town ball, where he pitched his team into the tournaments with his fastball. The photographer for the local paper could hardly catch that pitch with his flashbulb. Next the minor league scouts stood waiting for him after a game, their smiles like piano keys, and everything speeded up, as if someone had tilted the whole world and it started sliding toward him. A minor league coach watched him, chin on his hand, for three months in Class A, then, at midseason, the coach nodded at him once. The next day Dusty was moved up to Triple A, the bleachers bigger and more freshly painted, the fans louder. He kept moving up, faster and quicker. His life seemed to be rushing toward him and flying away from him at the same moment. His arm felt great, and the more he threw, the better it felt. The leather ball loved his fingertips. "The kid's so good he could pitch blindfolded and still strike out the side," a coach once remarked. On the mound, Dusty went through his motion: kicking, reaching way back in the still air with his right arm. Then he whirled down hard, and the ball was nestled in the catcher's mitt long before Dusty's cap, jolted from his head, had a chance to fall to the grass in front of the mound. The ball was like music that passed so fast you never really heard it.

He remembers the rush as he was called to the bigs: the flutter of a paper contract, the tingling static electricity as he slid a major league uniform over his head for the first time in the locker room, the click and spark of spikes on concrete as he jogged down the ramp to the dugout.

The next thing he knew, the game was starting, and the first batter stepped to the plate. Then, the funniest thing happened—everything slowed down. It took half an hour to reach up to adjust the bill of his cap. His windup felt like an elaborate dance performed underwater. When he threw that first pitch, the ball seemed to take a year to reach home plate, like some kind of satellite aimed for the moon, just rotating over and over slowly in the soft, endless vacuum of space.

Somehow, he made it through the first game and he did all

right. He pitched six innings, gave up a couple of hits, but no runs. Not bad for a first outing. The guys patted him on the back after the game. The catcher congratulated him and told him later how his eyes always widened each time he delivered the ball. He had a great year, and the papers called him the Rookie Sensation. The sportswriters always used the word *potential* when they wrote about him; they predicted he'd be the best in the game.

The seasons passed. One, two, three of them. He chalked up fifty wins. Then, one night in Chicago, too cool for June, when the bases were loaded in the late innings, he reached as far back as he could to fire a fastball and felt something snap in his arm. Not *snap*, exactly—it was more of a *ping*, like the off-key sound of a thin wire or guitar string being plucked. It didn't hurt at first, though he remembers shaking his arm a few times as if it had ants on it.

When he threw his next pitch, and the next, he knew something was wrong. The ball didn't quite go where it was aimed. Just an inch or two off target, but that's all it takes. He lost that game on a double. After that, the batters began hitting his curve, his slider. His fastball lost its jump, no longer appeared to be rising as it reached the batter, but instead drew a straight line to the sweet spot of their bats.

That's when the music slowed down, his career like a record clicked off in the middle of its playing, the needle dragging across the vinyl.

The team put him on the disabled list and he sat it out for a couple weeks. He worked with the trainer in the clubhouse, rotating the arm, wrapping it with heat, kneading the muscle as if it were bread dough about to rise. After he gave up six or seven runs in each of his next three starts, the manager shook his head and said the owners wanted him sent down to the minors.

"How long?" Dusty remembers asking the manager. He felt suddenly short of breath, unable to exhale a full sentence.

The manager stood chewing a toothpick, staring only at Dusty's arm. "Just a while. That's all. A month, maybe. You'll be back, kid."

"Yeah," he responded. "A month."

A month became the rest of the season. He struggled in the minors, too—even the rookies were hitting his best pitches, taking them to the gaudily painted wooden fences advertising CHEER and BRYLCREEM—A LITTLE DAB'LL DO YA, and COLGATE WITH GARDOL.

The next February, he got a letter from the club. He remembers staring at the outside of the long beige envelope that morning, not certain if he should open it or not. He set it down on the desk. He remembers watching TV for a while. The Colgate ad appeared—an announcer with a mike stood behind an invisible protective Gardol shield as a major league pitcher threw fastballs at him. The pitches bounced off the shield one by one. Dusty clicked the set off. After lunch, he picked the letter up again. As he tore it open, the ripping paper made the sound of crackling ice. The letter told him, in a few curt sentences, that his contract wouldn't be renewed. The last sentences read: *Thank you for your contribution to the club. Best wishes in the future.*

He remembers crumpling the letter in his fist, tossing it into the waste basket, and jogging out to the nearby sandlot field. Though it was cold outside and patches of ice still plastered themselves to the field, Dusty threw fastball after fastball toward the warped black and white plate, none of them strikes. The pain in his arm seemed to make a noise that grew louder and louder, like a scream caught beneath the skin.

*   *   *

The shrill sound of his alarm clock brings him back to his apartment. He jogs into the bedroom, clicks off the ringing alarm. All that was years ago, he thinks as he brushes his teeth, combs his graying slicked-back hair, slides on his snappy brown striped tie and brown suit jacket, then slips out the front door for work. He's got a new career, and he's a different man now—he's Dusty Sikarsky, best damn car salesman in El Dorado, Kansas. He's got his sales pitch down perfect, and he's got plaques on the wall of his office at Edge Motors and citations from the El Dorado Businessmen's Club to prove it. He's got a quick, bright smile on his face and the music in his voice; his boss once said he could sell any car on the lot blindfolded.

Dusty tastes the first warmth of April air as he walks through the town. It's a taste he's almost forgotten, a taste aromatic and rich that seems to come from deep inside the thawed earth and from deep inside himself at the same moment. By the time he reaches the low, tin-sided building at the car lot, he's puffing. He grins at his coworkers as he lopes toward his dark paneled office. Inside, as he waits for the first customer, he takes a wheezy drag from his cigarette, pours a mug of coffee, and, cupping a powdered sugar donut in his palm, stares beyond the hulls of the cars to the shimmering water mirage beginning to form at the far end of the asphalt lot.

The whole town seems to know about his days in the majors. As he walks down Main in front of the crumbling two-story brick facades, a little heavier and a little grayer, the kids open their eyes wide as they pass and then whisper behind him: "You know who *that* is? That's Dusty Sikarsky. He pitched in the majors." Some of the older guys at work smile and say, "Hey Dusty, what was it like, pitching in the big leagues?" Dusty usually just shakes his head. He wants to

reply, *What's there to say? You just throw a ball at a glove.*
But he doesn't want to sound flip so he just says something
pat like "Good. It was real good."

He never talks much about the big leagues, never mentions
the injury. For years now, he's managed to avoid talking
about it, has become adept at a subtle curve of conversation,
a change of subject. *Gardol,* he thought once after he dodged
a coworker's question about baseball, *an invisible protective
shield.* He never goes to the town league baseball games on
the weekends, though his buddies sometimes ask him to take
in a game. Once in a while, as a gag, he'll ball up an old
invoice, go into his windup, pitch it hard through the bright
light of the open doorway, and the guys nod at him and know
he remembers.

"You should pick up a baseball sometime, Dusty," the
boss told him once. "Ever think of coaching or something?"
Dusty just took a slurp of coffee, pretending not to hear.
"Cripes, with no wife, no kids," the boss added, "you got all
the time in the world."

His arm doesn't hurt like it used to the first couple years
after he was cut from the team. It only aches a little once in
a while as he lifts a pile of ledgers or when he leans his weight
the wrong way on the waxed fender of a Chevy while making
a pitch about what a workhorse the V6 engine is, how fast
this machine would be on the highway even though it's got
a few miles on the ol' speedometer.

This April day passes with its usual blur of stats and sales,
printouts and receipts. Another day passes beneath his fingertips and it feels dry to the touch. In the late afternoon, an
ad appears in the *El Dorado Weekly* proclaiming SHINY
CLEAN USED CARS FOR SPRING. In the picture, Dusty, pudgy
and not quite smiling, poses stiffly beside a Dodge, like he
doesn't know what to do with his hands.

*   *   *

After work, on his way home, Dusty takes a detour to the town ball field. Shouldering through the creaking fence gate, he pulls off his wide striped tie, unbuttons the top button of his white shirt. He sits down on the front row of the bleachers, slips off his brown suit jacket, tosses it over a corroded railing. He can hear the whistle of the wind through the high backstop, a rusty music. He sits there a while, gazing at the empty sunlit field from behind the barrier of wires. Rolling up his sleeves, he massages the muscle of his right arm. Then he notices, directly behind the plate, widened gaps in the backstop wires. *A wild pitch could get caught in there easy,* Dusty thinks. *It could get caught for years between the bent wires.*

Turning his head, Dusty notices two boys biking across the grass. He thinks at first that they're cutting across the field on their way to the video games at the arcade, but they stop in the middle of the infield. One skinny kid who looks about seven keeps trying to pitch from the gravelly mound sixty feet away, but can't quite get his throws to home plate. He hefts the ball like a shotput, and the ball skitters in the dirt a few feet from the plate where another boy, short and chunky, stands with a catcher's mitt that's too big for his hand. The boy who's pitching moves a few steps closer. An idea crosses Dusty's mind that he should go out there and give the kid a few tips. The kid brings his arm down pretty well, but he's bending all wrong at the elbow. *Naw,* he thinks. *Let the kids have their game.* The boy tosses another one, a rounded throw that skips in front of the catcher's mitt, rolls all the way to the backstop.

The skinny kid runs from the mound to retrieve it. By the

time the boy reaches the backstop, Dusty is stretching his arm through the bent wires to pick up the baseball, snagging the sleeve of his white shirt on a sharp, loose wire.

"You stuck, mister?" the kid asks.

Dusty smiles up at the boy from his knees.

"Nope," Dusty blurts. "Yeah. I mean, I don't know."

A little embarrassed, Dusty manages a chuckle. Still clutching the baseball, he hears something in the sleeve tear as he pulls his arm back. *It's okay*, he thinks, *you can replace a shirt. You can put a Band-Aid on a scratched arm.*

He stands with the ball, faces the boy through the wires, and grins. The boy cups his hands as if expecting Dusty to toss the ball over, as if expecting a brief spring shower. But Dusty doesn't toss the ball. Instead, he finds himself stepping through a gate in the fence, hears his voice ask, "Wanna learn some pitches?" Instead, Dusty finds himself slipping off his polished shoes and brown dress socks, then climbing the small mountain of the pitcher's mound, all that gravel suddenly tender and welcoming beneath his bare feet.

Things Are Always
So Close

His face is tanned like the ballplayers', but he never looks as handsome. He stands on the field beneath the same sky as they do, but he never looks as lean or graceful. Pitch by pitch, the ball comes right at him, slaps in the catcher's mitt, and everyone waits for him to make the call. Between innings, he glances up at the clouds for the chances of rain. The chances of rain are always good and bad. For an umpire, things are always on the border like that.

Roger always wears his basic uniform, a blue shirt and gray polyester pants with the wide legs that flap when the wind blows. He wears the chest protector, the heavy mask that keeps him from everybody else. He's dressed for the game each day, but he knows he never looks sharp like the players with their pinstriped casualness, their knicker pants hiked up over flashy red or blue socks. He just blends into the background, and that's where an umpire should stay, he tells himself. He's background, but he's what keeps the game moving forward with each call: out, safe, strike, ball.

On the next pitch the batter hits a grounder to short, and the runner tries to score. It's a close play at home, and the runner slides toward the plate and into the catcher's mitt. "Yer out!" Roger bellows, making a gesture as if he were throwing his fist off his arm and into the sky. After the call, the manager charges from the dugout and argues. But Roger simply states the facts to the manager, whose chin is two inches from him. "The left foot never touched home," Roger repeats calmly. *Control,* he thinks. *Keep the peace.* Then he turns and begins dusting off the plate. The manager keeps yelling at his back, but Roger shuts his mind off. *You have to be fair,* he thinks. *Level. Fair. You have to. You can't explode just because they do. Face it. Face the difficulty. Make the choice. Then dust off the damn home plate so it's ready for another call.*

Roger knows it's a tough world, being an umpire. Between innings you scan the faces in the crowd as if looking for someone you recognize. But you never find them, of course. You don't know anybody. Nobody loves you—not batter, nor pitcher, nor fan. Nobody wants to talk to you after the game, either. The players shake hands with one another or pat one another on the shoulder, but they don't care about the ump. He could be invisible, for all they care. He could be the shapeless curl of smoke rising from a manager's cigarette when he lights up in disgust after losing a game.

After the stands clear, Roger stands behind the trunk of his car in the parking lot, silently unbuttoning his blue shirt, slipping it into the duffel bag marked NEBRASKA CENTRAL VALLEY LEAGUE, while the players stroll past and climb into a bouncing team bus, the winners talking and laughing and dropping candy wrappers from the open windows.

He slides into his car, clicks on the ignition. When he hears a song on the radio that reminds him of his wife, Theresa, he sits a moment, listening. The Chordettes are warbling: "Mister Sandman, bring me a dream. . . ." *That harmony,* he thinks. He remembers how, in their younger days, he and Theresa danced to that song out at their favorite bar, The Gully. He decides to forget the motel room he reserved in this town for after the game. He decides to drive home instead of staying overnight like he told his wife. Then, for an instant, he catches himself wondering: Will she be there when he gets home? He pushes the doubt from his mind, listens to the rest of the song. "Please please bring me a dream." *Their voices are so clear on that harmony,* he thinks, *they sound just like bells ringing.*

Pulling out of the parking lot, he thinks about this game he's just finished. Strikes, and balls, and split-second calls. You have to be alert as anything if you're an ump, you can never be drowsy, and you can never blink at the wrong time or you might miss something. It makes him feel important to think that if he blinks, he'll miss something. Early in his career he'd sometimes practice keeping his eyes wide for a few seconds, training himself not to blink. Because one thing an umpire can't do is guess. You can never guess, or you're washed up.

"Sometimes I think I *am* going blind, like they say," he said to his wife a few weeks ago, laughing.

"Yeah" was all she replied.

He heard somewhere that in leagues like this, an umpire is allowed three mistakes per game, but he's not sure he believes it anymore. He worries a lot lately. When he reads the sports section in the paper, he focuses on the close games, and he hopes the ump made the right calls. He's been in those games decided by one pitch on the outside corner, one runner nipped by a quarter-step at first base. He knows the feeling when the hometown crowd gets on you, and you can feel all that yelling and name-calling stinging your back. "Come on, ump!" they'll shout. "Goddammit, he was safe." Or: "You blind bastard! That was a strike and you know it!" The worst feeling for an umpire is when the whole game hinges on one call. He'd rather the game ended on a play that had nothing to do with the ump, like a base hit to center or a long home run.

He worries sometimes about whether he made the right call. The older he gets, the more he notices how close everything is. Life is like that—everything's tentative, on the edge of something else: There's water or there's land, there's silence or there's noise, there's waking or sleeping, there's life or there's death.

As he drives on the highway, he thinks back to his first year as an umpire, to that play at the plate he's never forgotten. He was just eighteen, barely older than the Babe Ruth League kids he umpired for in the city leagues. He remembers standing behind home plate with that big, air-filled chest protector they used in those days. A ball would bounce off that big blue heart-shaped barrier like it was bouncing off a trampoline. When he first started umping, he felt infallible, like the protector could stop a bullet fired at him at point blank range. He envisions that play again: bases loaded, two out, and a full count on the batter. As the pitcher began his slow windup, the runner from third broke toward the plate to steal home. He was a quick runner, and he got there just as the ball did, but he didn't slide. He came in standing up, and as his left leg stepped on the plate, the pitch hit him in the hip. It would have been strike three. Roger remembers the confusion like pool balls scattering to the sides of a table after a cue-ball break: Did the pitch count? Wasn't that interference by the runner? But wasn't the runner safe because his foot was on the plate when the pitch came in? The batter couldn't have swung at the pitch with a man standing on the plate. Should the run score, or was it a called strike three? He had no rule book, and no other ump was around to advise him. The batter, catcher, runner, and pitcher all stared at him as he just blinked and hesitated. They waited for him to make the call, and Roger felt numb and foolish, just standing there, unable to move or say a word. He felt like he was caught in a net of silence, an umpire's hell. He just stared straight ahead at the field as long seconds passed. Finally, the batter dropped the bat, breaking the statuelike pose everyone held on the field. Then the rest of the players began to move. The team at bat—perhaps assuming they'd done something wrong—picked up their equipment and headed onto the field and the other team slowly walked off as if the inning was over. No one said a word to Roger or to each other. That was the strangest thing about it. As if everyone understood, *no one said a word.* At home that night, Roger couldn't sleep because of that play. He kept seeing that runner's foot stomp on the plate at the moment the ball struck him. He kept seeing his own face, paralyzed, indecisive behind the thick black aluminum bars of that mask.

Roger looks at a road sign and sees that it's another hundred miles to his home. He checks his wristwatch—it's ten o'clock. If he hurries and keeps it at seventy, he'll be there by eleven-thirty. He'll surprise his wife, and maybe tell her a little about the game. Or maybe he'll talk to her about that play his first year as an ump when he was so indecisive. He'll tell her he won't let that happen again. He knows she hates it when he's indecisive and can't make up his mind. He'll tell her he's changed. Or maybe he won't talk to her, just wake her gently from sleep by rubbing her shoulder, bare beneath the strap of her red nightgown. Then he'll slide his arms around her and kiss her. Maybe he won't talk to her at all, just kiss her, and make love to her, and that'll be enough.

He stares at the blinking lines in the road and thinks about how, his first year of umping, after that play at the plate, he went to the library and got all the rule books he could and studied them, memorizing every situation possible in a game, just so he'd be ready. He didn't want anything like that to happen to him again in his career: that feeling of being frozen, like a man caught inside the ice of a glacier. During his research, he read that the difference between a major leaguer and a minor leaguer is a hundredth of a second. Whether it be fielding or batting, that little difference separates the pros from the scrubs. You have the reflexes down right, and you've got it all. Whether you swing the bat or lunge for a ball at short, that's all it takes. And for umps, it's different, but, in a way, the same. It's the tiniest distances, the tiniest of moments that count the most. It's a hundredth of an inch. It's a hundredth of a second when a runner's foot is about to touch first base and the throw from third's an inch from the fielder's mitt. And you have to be on the right side of that hundredth of an inch or hundredth of a second. You've got to be accurate, or you might as well forget it. *You have to be fair. In control.* You have to have your perceptions filed sharp to a point.

Things are so close, after all. He worries about it. Worries whether or not his reactions are starting to die now that he's almost forty. Though you wouldn't know it from his stocky build and the way his gray polyester pants seem tighter around the waist each day, he's still young. He doesn't want those reactions to die, doesn't want to start blinking at the moment the pitch comes across the plate. He met a fellow in the River League who, one afternoon over a few beers, told him about the time he was hit in the throat with a foul tip. It hurt bad when he got hit, he explained; it stung the rest of the game, and he couldn't shake it off. From then on, he started blinking at each pitch, a kind of unconscious flinch, almost, and so he had trouble calling balls and strikes. He couldn't help but thinking, after that foul tip, *Where there's one, there's others coming.* The fellow lost his job a couple months later, after he couldn't make the right calls and he got too many complaints from both managers in some games. "If you're going to be an ump," the hiring office told him, "you've got to make a high percentage of good calls. Simple as that. If not, you're washed up."

It begins to rain as Roger takes the turn onto the county road. The first wide splatters hit the windshield, which is nicked with bug marks. He waits a few seconds until he clicks on the wipers.

Roger worries a little about his wife. He worries that she might be playing around on him when he's gone to these evening games. Sometimes he has to stay overnight for two or three days during a tournament up near the state line, or when he heads over to South Dakota for some league play-off.

The first time he knew something was wrong was when he drove home early from a Saturday night game that was called because the electrical generator went out on the field, and they had no lights. He thought he'd get back by nine, maybe in time to take his wife out to dinner. When he walked in the door, he stood in the kitchen and he knew by the way the room smelled that she was gone. It was the faint, wafting scent of her Chanel perfume, a perfume she hadn't worn with him for years. It was lingering on the wooden kitchen cupboards, on the walls, around the wooden table. He could almost see it, like tiny scented tightropes wafting in the air.

He drove through town and spotted Theresa's car at The Gully. The place was a converted motel; after the motel went bankrupt, the new owner boarded up several of the rooms and remodeled the office into a bar. Roger remembers pulling his car next to Theresa's pink and cream Buick with the four holes in the side.

He opened his door quickly and stood there a moment, watching the cloud of dust from his car settle across the chrome of the Buick, taking away its shine.

Before he even opened the screen door to The Gully, he heard her laughter and he knew. He held that door open halfway and stood half in the darkness, half in the light. He pictured everything in the bar—the bluish, smoky air, the pool table in one corner, the knotty pine walls, the lit Hamm's beer sign behind the bar, with the trout jumping high out of the water. Then he looked up to where her laughter—a sound like glasses clinking together—was coming from. He saw long brown hair flowing down the back of her pink blouse as she sat in a booth. Across from her, in the booth, sat a smiling man. Roger had a notion to walk in, pull her from the booth, then swing his fist and knock the man against the wall. He had a notion. He had a notion to just pull her up to him and kiss her. But instead, he just stood there, hesitating, holding the splintered wood frame of the screen door and staring at the back of her head, as if that blind stare of his was enough to make her turn around. But she didn't turn around, didn't feel his stare, so all he could do was let go of the door and walk back to his Chevy. He jumped into the car and floored it out of the parking lot, gravel sputtering behind him.

When she got home that night, he was sitting at the table in the unlit kitchen.

"What are you doing back so early?" Theresa asked.

"Game was called," he said, slowly raising his eyes from the table to look at her.

"Why?"

He stood up and slid his fingers around her arm. She seemed nervous, embarrassed. "No lights," he replied.

"No lights?" she repeated. He could smell the beer on her breath, and her hair smelled stale, smoke mixed with her Chanel perfume.

"And where were you?" he asked, trying to sound casual.

"Out."

"Out? That's all you can say?"

She walked past him, her arm brushing his chest. "That's what I said, didn't I? Out. What is it with you, Roger?" She opened the refrigerator door, squinted as the bright light fell across her and onto the floor in a triangle.

He walked up to her, turned her toward him. "How long you been doing this when I've been gone?"

"Doing what?" she asked, giggling, trying to seem innocent.

"You know what I mean."

"I don't have the slightest idea," she said evasively. "I was out with friends. I don't spend every night waiting for you to come home from some ball game. I have friends, you know." She sauntered into the bedroom, clicked the door shut tight behind her.

He stood, staring at the closed wooden door of their bedroom, and he didn't know what to say. He wanted to yell something at the hollow-core door, but he didn't know what. So he just opened his mouth and let a sound slide out, and all it sounded like was *awwwwww*. The sound got gradually louder, until he was shouting it, making the wood vibrate. After a few seconds, she opened the door, just a crack, and the light cut through the dark kitchen like a yellow pane of glass. Her face appeared in the opening, and he could tell she was angry. "Damn it, Roger, if you're going to say something, then do me a favor. Don't bellow at me like an umpire. Say it in English, so I can understand it."

He knew she was a little drunk, and that she didn't really mean it. But the thing was, she was right. He didn't know how to say it. He could never get his emotions in line so he could explain them, not to anyone, not even to himself. They were just somewhere inside him, massive and coiling, and all he could do was get angry. If he was at a ball game, and he had a logical argument, he could raise his voice in a controlled way, like he did with any barking manager or fuming player after a close play. He could raise his voice and say just what was needed. "He didn't touch home. He didn't touch home." No matter how many times the coach or player shouted, "Yes he did!" he'd return in a clear, controlled voice: "I said he didn't touch home." But this was different. He stood there, facing the layer of wood in the darkness, knowing he didn't understand her at all, and he simply didn't know what to say.

That was a year ago. Things seemed better between them for a while, but the past few weeks, she'd seemed upset with him again. "You've got to talk more," she pleaded with him during one argument, "tell me your feelings. What's in your heart, your gut. Not just how long the game lasted or what the scores were, but how you *felt*. You've got to communicate more with me, Roger. Do you know what I mean?" He nodded his head yes, though he wasn't exactly sure what she meant.

Now the windshield wipers do their slapslap dance on the glass in front of him, clearing, for a moment, his vision that splatters and blurs, splatters and blurs.

His headlights glare off the city limits sign and his car seems to crawl through his hometown as if the tires are sticking to the wet streets. Will she be gone, he wonders, will she be out at the bar with somebody? Will she be at home, watching TV like she sometimes does? He's not certain. He can't guess. As he drives closer, he regrets that he didn't call her long distance from the ballpark.

He clicks the headlights off, pulls the car up the driveway in front of his small house. The gravel under the tires makes a sound like a catcher in the distance, popping his fist in his mitt. He sees no light through the windows of the Rambler. *She's gone out,* he thinks. *Damn it, she's out.* The thought stings him like a foul tip. *You're washed up, buddy, washed up.*

He sits in the car a few seconds with the motor off. Images from the final play of the game that night flash through his mind. The home team was behind by a run, and their big cleanup hitter was up. On a three-and-two pitch, the pitcher threw one on the inside corner. The ball broke in a little bit, a slider, and the batter leaned back off the plate. Roger wasn't certain for a moment what to call. Not certain at all.

The next thing he knows he's walking up the front sidewalk to his house. He's turning his key in the latch, unlocking the door with his key, stepping into the darkened kitchen. He hears movement inside the bedroom. The bedroom door's wide open but the room is unlit. Thinks he hears a hushed voice. One voice, or two? *No,* he thinks, she's talking in her sleep, the way she does sometimes. He steps to the doorway and he can't really see, but there seems to be a motion, sort of, with covers and sheets moving. Is she waking up? Is she tossing in her sleep? Or is she trying to hide? Standing inside that doorway he hesitates. In that moment he doesn't want to know. For a moment he's safe, not knowing.

He can't guess what he might be about to see, or what

relief or pain is waiting to engulf him. Maybe it won't be fair. Maybe nothing's fair.

With a deep breath, he's ready, ready for whatever the game wants to deal out, whatever call life is about to give him. And he feels better, just because of that, just because he knows he can't be the one to decide this time. He lets go. *No control.*

"Theresa," he whispers. It's the only word he can say right now. "Theresa." He says it a third time, this time with feeling: "Theresa." No matter what happens, he knows it's going to be close. After all, with him and his wife, things are always so close.

The Unwinding

Chasing a moth from the backstop to the edge of the woods, my five-year-old son finds it: an old baseball. He sees it beneath the fallen leaves, muddied and half-submerged in the soil like the top of some large, ancient snail shell.

He lifts the ball, and, holding it above his head, runs to show me his discovery. We stand near home plate of the baseball diamond, turning the ball over and over in our palms. The ball's leather cover has been eaten away, perhaps seasons ago, by the teeth of rain and snow. Now all that's left is the water-heavy core of wound string that has been sinking slowly into the earth year after year.

"I have an idea," he tells me. He finds the loose end of string, pinches it between his fingertips. "I could unroll this string and find out what's inside. Can I try it?"

"Sure, I guess you could," I tell him, and as I say this I recall unraveling the strings of baseballs when I was a boy in Wisconsin. I picture a length of string that seemed miles long. I used to find the torn, waterlogged balls in deep weeds at the edge of the Baraboo River just beyond the high school practice field. You could get to the strings by shucking off the rotted leather cover, which pulled free like the loosened shell of a hard-boiled egg.

What did I ever find in the center of those baseballs? Perhaps it was a cork ball, perhaps it was a tiny rubber sphere. Or maybe it was just string unreeling into nothing. I don't recall what I found—I only remember the unraveling, the pile of musty-smelling string at my feet, a few strands wound around my ankles.

My son grasps the free end of the string and begins to unroll the ball as I stretch my legs and arms to warm up.

He backs up while pulling the string, then walks across the diamond and around the backstop. He grasps the string tightly in one fist, chuckling to himself, as if he were holding on to a kite string, or a line leading to his first caught fish. The ball, near the pitcher's mound, rotates and wobbles nervously in place as it plays out string inch by inch.

"Is it getting smaller?" he asks me.

"Yes, it is," I answer. I watch the ball, which seems to spin around on its own crazy axis. When I was young, my friends and I unwound the baseballs by the river while we fished. We didn't get much action in that slow, muddy river, except for an occasional catch of a bullhead, so we had time to prop our poles in the notches of sticks planted in the mud, lie down in the grass and unreel the baseballs. I remember thinking, as a young boy, how our small town's river flowed into the Wisconsin River, and the Wisconsin into the Mississippi, and the Mississippi flowed all the way to the ocean. Once we put notes in bottles, tossed them into the center of the river, watched them float downstream. We daydreamed they'd carry all the way to the sea. One spring—I must have been ten years old then—I hooked a big fish on my line. The spool of line spun quickly. I leaped up from the grass, grabbed the pole, and the lunker fish jumped, sending up a crystal wing of water. At that moment my line snapped, and the fish pulled it into the middle of the river.

* * *

"What will we find when we get to the center?" my son asks as he continues to walk with the string.

"I don't know," I answer. "Just keep rolling it, and we'll see."

"But what if it's empty inside?"

"What do you mean?"

He stands still a moment. "What if all the string unwinds and there's nothing there?"

I crouch down and look him in the eye. "Not possible," I assure him, and I hope I'm right.

He shuffles backward in the grass, watching the ball intently as he does. The gray string is a darker color near the middle of the ball.

I toss my five new baseballs into the air and stroke some fly balls toward the outfield. As I jog out to retrieve the balls, I see him, farther down the first-base line. He's spinning slowly, rolling the string around his waist like he's a spool.

"Look, Daddy," he calls. "I'm a baseball, too."

I nod at him, return with the baseballs, and hit another round. By the time I jog back, my son's already far beyond the right-field fence and into the adjoining baseball field; there are six diamonds scattered on the acres of this park. He seems to be walking faster, spinning slightly as he does.

Then I look down and notice that his ball is not unwinding. It's motionless near the dust of the pitcher's mound. Running close to the ball, I peer at it to be sure, and discover that the string has broken at a thin spot; the end of the long string my son holds is gliding away through the grass, a thin yarn snake.

I call his name. I call it again, louder. But he's already five hundred feet away and can't hear me; wind blowing hard toward home plate keeps my voice from carrying to him.

I lean forward and shout as loudly as I can.

"Wait!" I shout, waving one arm. "Come back! The string's broken."

He simply grins, waves to me, and keeps walking farther and farther.

I strain my eyes to see him now, my vision not what it used to be. He's beyond the fence of the second baseball diamond, shrinking smaller until he's only a dot on the horizon. "Come back!" I shout once more, and I wait for his reply. I think I hear his tiny voice wafting on the wind, like the song of a distant bird in flight, but I'm not certain. I wait, cupping one hand around my ear. Maybe all I hear is the sound of the wind rushing past my cupped hand—the sound an aging man hears when he puts his ear to an empty seashell and believes he hears the whole ocean inside.

The Here and Now

Herb's glasses are cracked from diving for fast grounders when he plays on his over-forty softball league, and he tapes the bridge of the thick brown plastic frames with white adhesive tape. If you stare at him, his eyes, magnified, look much larger than they really are.

Ever since January, he's been watching reruns on the snow-blurred TV set. He's been watching *Green Acres* and *Bewitched* and *Gilligan's Island* and he has the Body Shaper 5000 commercial memorized. It's the end of February, and he leans forward on the edge of the sofa and thinks, *Now*. He knows there's a field waiting for him out there, a field somewhere in the South where the weather has already warmed, a field where the grass blades rise like green whispers from the soil, and he feels the impulse to stand in the middle of his living room. He stands in the middle of his living room. Then he clicks off the announcer's nasal voice as he begins the Body Shaper 5000 litany again.

Herb opens the front door, peers outside, sees the snow still on the lawn. He scratches the stubble on the side of his face. *Damn winter*, he thinks. *Up north, in winter, I feel just like Gilligan trying to get off that island.*

He hurries to the closet, rummages through his ski mask and unmatched Thinsulate gloves, pulls out his duffel bag and slides on a pair of jogging pants and a wrinkled, hole-spattered T-shirt that's too tight for him. Then he takes his shirts and pants off the hangers and stuffs them into the bag. He finds his grease-stained baseball cap, flabby and deflated on a shelf. He pulls it on, feels it filling with all the ideas in his head. When he turns, his wife is standing behind him, watching.

"What are you doing?" Delores asks. "Dressing for the prom?"

He bends toward her and takes a slight bow.

"Answer me, Herb. Where are you planning to go?"

"Just to a field somewhere," he says offhandedly. "In Florida, I mean."

She notices that his eyes look much larger than they really are. "Sure, Herb," she scoffs. "That's eighteen hundred miles away."

"Here," Herb says with a sly grin, locking arms with Delores and pulling her. "Take a step." They step forward from the closet.

"Herb . . ." Delores laughs.

"Now," says Herb, raising his voice as if he's announcing a special event. "It's two feet closer."

"What?" she says. "The TV?"

"No. Florida. So," he says, his voice inflating in the room. "Are we going or not?"

Delores thinks for a while. "Maybe," she finally says. "As long as I get to Disney World this time." She's bargaining now, but she knows it might work. "And to some of the souvenir shops." She glances down at the green and gold shag carpet. "And maybe a trip to the ocean." The last time they went south together, they only got as far as Chattanooga, Tennessee, and she never got anywhere near Orlando.

"Aren't you a little old for Disney?" he asks, though he already knows the answer.

"Are you kidding?" she says. "I've wanted to go there since I was a little girl. It's for adults, too, you know."

She's heard all about Florida and Disney World and the shell shops from her friends in bridge club. She imagines places called Shell World and Treasures of the Sea. Acres and acres of shells. Conchs, spiny shells, smooth polished shells, all kinds of them. Picture frames made of coral and shells. Table coasters with sea horses suspended inside the clear plastic.

"So," she asks. "Are we going or not?"

They're in a train somewhere, traveling south. When he gets there, Herb thinks, he'll rent a car, travel from town to town to see the baseball fields—any field will do, minor league, even Class C fields or some decent town fields. Delores sits next to him, wearing her Minnie Mouse T-shirt she bought at a blue light special at Kmart. Herb watches as a brown-framed snapshot of America slides past outside the window: Great fields stretch to the horizon like sheets pulled taut. The low buildings of small towns slowly rise, then slowly shrink on the landscape. A water tower balances itself on stilts. Truck stop signs, perched high, try to attract travelers like lures at the tips of fishing poles. A frayed plastic bag cartwheels in the wind, then clings to a lone telephone pole. Herb shifts his gaze straight ahead, feeling the vibration of the rails beneath him, imagining the color of the sky above the train. He'd rather be in a Great Western boxcar, sitting there in the echoing hollow, his duffel bag strapped over one arm, his baseball cap tipped back on his forehead. He'd rather be back there, watching through the open boxcar door: Outside, he'd see an empty ball field, the light posts surrounding it. Soon, the field will fill with players.

Delores leans back on the stiff cloth seat of the train and

closes her eyes. She'd rather be on the Tomorrowland Monorail, circling Disney World. That Monorail would glide so smoothly, you'd hardly know you were moving. She can picture the park below: the swarming crowds, the brightly colored concessions, the huge castle with its glistening spires jutting into the air, the colored flags waving in the wind at Fantasyland, the Mad Hatter's Teacups spinning and spinning and spinning.

He'd rather be in that boxcar, watching the countryside blur past him as though it were in motion and he was sitting stark still. He'd rather be waiting for the train to come to a jerking halt somewhere in a freight yard at dusk. He can almost smell the smoke from the barrel fires of the hoboes at the far end of the yard, hear the fading laughter of the railroad men as they hop from the engine or caboose and crunch through the gravel to the station. He'd rather be in that boxcar, slipping his arms around his wife, who would be dressed in a torn T-shirt and faded baseball cap, too. *Baseball bums,* he thinks. She'd be wearing a shell necklace around her neck. He'd rather be leaning back with her in a kiss, resting their heads on the duffel bag. He'd rather be kissing her and slipping her faded Sundogs T-shirt over her head, noticing the tiny sparks of static electricity that flicker from the fabric. Sleep wouldn't matter. In the still night air, he'd hear the thundering sound of the trains coupling and uncoupling all night.

"Want to get something at the club car?" his wife's voice asks, interrupting his vision.

"What?" He opens his eyes, a little dazed at his comfortable surroundings.

"The club car. Want to get some food?"

"No," he blurts. "No."

"Well I'm hungry," she says.

He takes her hand in his. "So am I," he says.

* * *

Late in the day, the train pulls to a stop just beyond the wooden sign WELCOME TO ALGONA, GATEWAY TO CENTRAL IOWA. Herb and Delores leave the train. He carries his duffel bag in one hand, the mashed clothes inside making it look rounded. With his other hand, he carries her gray Samsonite suitcase packed full with pantsuits and shoes and cosmetics and whatever it is she keeps in there. As he steps off the train, Herb notices the layer of snow on the yards, sniffs at the cool air. *No more than thirty,* he thinks. Across from the station, they stop at a Kwik Mart for bathrooms and snacks. Faint country music whines from a countertop radio next to a rack of postcards depicting silos and barns. In the bathroom, Herb notices a wall dispenser advertising The Sex Kit, featuring "His and Hers Swedish Massage Oils." He drops three quarters into the dispenser, tucks a kit into the pocket of his brown polyester pants. When he steps outside, Delores is holding a pale yellow Little Debbie marshmallow pie wrapped in clear cellophane. Herb pays for the pie and his packet of CornNuts, and they walk down the wide main street toward a motel.

"This," says Delores, as she takes a bite of the pie, "is heavenly." She pulls off a gooey piece for Herb, and he chews it obligingly.

"If I ever strike it rich," she says, "I'm going to buy a million of these."

"If you ever strike it rich as an Avon lady," Herb counters with a chuckle, "I'll be president of General Motors."

They check into the motel called the Gateway Motel and Bait Shop. The hand-painted GATEWAY sign next to the building features cows standing by a fence with the gate slightly open. Below that are the words SPEND A NIGHT IN OUR PASTURE. Inside, Herb inspects the furnishings: a bolted-down black-

and-white TV, a mounted coffeepot in the corner, complete
with packets of Courtesy Coffee and Coffee Swirl, a framed
print of an ocean shoreline on one mahogany-paneled wall and
Elvis in Vegas on the other. The room's smell is a blend of stale
smoke and Fantastik. A tin shower stall squeezes next to the
sink in the bathroom. On the paper shower mat, two sea horses
face the hole for the drain. The mat advertises, in faded gold
letters, THE WANDER INN BAR—BEST BAR IN ALGONA, IOWA.
Delores opens the vinyl room-darkening drapes that cover the
picture window. Outside, there's a view of a John Deere outlet
with the rows of green tractors stretching to the stubble corn at
the edge of the lot. For some reason, Herb loves the whole
place, because it seems right. He yearns for the future, for its
promise, but he loves the here and now, too. He loves the here
and now, takes whatever it offers, because it's here. Now.

Delores shakes her head. "This isn't exactly a Disney re-
sort," she says. "I don't know why I let you talk me into
this."

"Because it's perfect, that's why," Herb replies.

At the Wander Inn, they sit on chrome and red vinyl chairs
at a table in the middle of the bar, their paunchy stomachs
pressing against the worn edge of the wood.

Behind the bar on a warped wooden shelf, next to a stuffed
bass with its mouth wide open, a row of softball trophies
glistens faintly in the dim light. Next to them, inside gallon
jars with corroded screw-on caps, pickled eggs and pale giz-
zards float, suspended in a cloudy liquid. A fellow in overalls
plays pool by himself at a table where the felt is worn through
in spots. In the corner, a dusty jukebox plays a scratchy
medley of songs by Boxcar Willie. At one point, the record
skips, and the fellow with overalls strolls to it, kicks it once
with his boot, and the record jumps ahead.

Herb glances at his wife. "Great atmosphere," he says with a smile. "Best bar in Algona, Iowa."

"*Only* bar in Algona, Iowa," Delores states.

He orders two Grain Belt tap beers and two shots of Wild Turkey.

"Here's what you do," he says. He takes a sip of the beer so it's down an inch from the rim, then lifts the shot of whiskey and drops shot glass and all into the tap. The beer fizzes and foams. Then he drinks the whole thing down quickly, wipes his mouth with the sleeve of his white Lake Okoboji T-shirt.

"Now that's refreshment," Herb says, grinning at his wife. He studies the pale yellow flecks in her irises.

"I don't drink whiskey," she replies.

"In that case, do you know what a Swedish massage is?" he asks.

She takes a long sip from her plain beer. "No," she says, "as a matter of fact I don't." She stands up to put another quarter in the jukebox.

Back at the motel, they lie down to the curve of the soft double bed, and its springs encourage them to roll toward each other in the middle. They lie down to the soft snowy hiss of the TV set. They sleep to the glow of the red and green neon lights that buzz intermittently on the overhang outside the room.

For a moment Herb has flickering dreams that he's in the boxcar again, a warm wind rippling his shirt. He reaches over, massages the middle of Delores's back. Her face turns and she kisses him with a deep kiss, and when the flickering stops he knows he's not dreaming anymore. He feels something rising like sap inside him and he's awake in a room that's not moving and he feels her breathing on his neck as they embrace. Her breath smells like beer and marshmallows. "I lied," her voice whispers. "I *do* know what a Swedish massage is."

In the morning, she steps from the shower, wrapped in a blue striped towel printed with the faded words GATEWAY MOTEL AND BAIT SHOP. The steam swirls around the ringlets of her wet, permed hair. "I hope you remembered last night," she says. "I didn't know if you were awake or asleep."

"Last night?" he says, raising his eyebrows. "What do you mean, last night?"

"Oh come on," she says, shaking her head.

"Don't worry," he says. "I never forget a thing, no matter if I'm asleep or not." He rolls up his striped pajamas and stuffs them in the duffel.

She dresses and waits for him to snap the suitcase shut. He sits on the Samsonite, latches it. "Isn't this the kind of suitcase that apes can't break in a zoo, even if they throw them around?" he asks.

She ignores him, pursing her lips, dabbing on her lipstick in front of the cracked mirror.

The cool morning winds swirl as they walk to the train depot.

"What's the temp supposed to be here today?" Herb asks the man wearing a blue uniform in the ticket booth.

The man looks at him from beneath the black vinyl brim of his cap. "Oh, I dunno. High of twenty-five, maybe thirty."

"Forget it," Herb says.

"Ain't exactly Orlando," his wife agrees with a scoff.

"Two tickets," he demands.

"Where to?" the uniformed man asks.

"South," he replies. "Someplace warm."

Herb hefts his wife's suitcase toward the baggage cart with a grunt.

"What've you got in here, anyway?" he asks Delores.

"Nothing," she says, "that an ape couldn't lift."

They ride the train, and the hangover from the whiskey and the short night's sleep catch up on Herb. *At our age, everything catches up on you,* he thinks. He leans his head back and dozes. He'll sleep an hour, even two. Maybe by that time, when he wakes, he'll be in baseball country. When he wakes, his eyes will comb the landscape like a blind man's fingers reading braille. He wants to start with some of the Class A games in Tennessee or maybe Georgia. He wants to visit every park in the league. His mind fizzes and foams at the thought.

In a few seconds, he's in that boxcar again. He's staring out through the open rectangular door. Outside that door, one by one, he sees all the parks in that Class A league pass by him—their wood-beam grandstands, their rusted foul poles, their splintered scoreboards, and their whitewashed concession stands—with nicked ordering counters held up by chains—where they sell taffy and Nibs and pop. He sees those ballplayers take the field in their rumpled, mothball-scented uniforms, sees the outfield lights on low poles illuminating an infield that was never lit so brightly in its life. Sees himself taking the field with a hustling bunch of young players, players with names like Stringer and Lefty and Whip and Youngblood. He jogs across the infield to his place at short to warm up. His glasses aren't taped, and they're kept secure on his face with an elastic band that hugs his skull. He fields a grounder to his left, fires it to first. One of the players, Young-blood, steps over to him. "Nice throw, Ace," he says, and he nudges Herb with his elbow.

Delores's elbow nudges him again and the dream quickly drains from him. "Herb? You're not going to sleep all day, are you?"

"Huh?" Herb says, shaking his groggy head.

"I slept a few minutes, too," she says. "Aren't you going to ask me if I had any dreams?"

"Did you have any dreams?" he says obediently.

"As a matter of fact, I did. I dreamt of a place called Shell Kingdom. You should have seen it. Acres of shells. The ocean was right out back, and I walked up to a shell on the beach. It was so big that I stepped into it and it started to spin and I rode it, just like the Mad Hatter's Teacup ride. I felt just like Alice in Wonderland." She stares at his half-closed lids a moment. "What were you dreaming, anyway?"

He shrugs, knowing the baseball dream wouldn't be anything new for her.

"You were fidgeting and jumping all over the place in your sleep." She points to his forehead. "What have you got in there, anyway?"

"Nothing, really," he replies. "I travel light."

They ride the train all afternoon, and into the night, and this time, instead of stopping at a town, they decide to sleep in the dormered bunks of the sleeping car. They climb into their bunks, and to Herb it feels like they're on their own separate island. He closes his eyes as the train shakes him. He doesn't know what they'll find tomorrow, doesn't know where they'll be when he opens his eyes. Maybe, with luck, when he opens them, they'll be somewhere in Florida, and it will already be baseball season there. Maybe, when Delores opens her eyes, she'll see a place like Shell Kingdom, and not too far from that, she'll see waves cartwheeling onto the sands of an endless beach.

From the lower bunk, Herb talks to his wife in the upper bunk before they fall asleep. They speak in low, murmuring tones, tones that almost blend in with the steady rumble of the train. They talk about the future, about where everything is going, and how fast, and about how they're both a little afraid. Sometimes he wishes they could just hold still, like those sea horses suspended in plastic.

"Promise me that you'll always take this trip with me," he says. "Next year. And the year after. Promise me you will." He utters the words softly, like a lover whispering sweet compliments.

She doesn't answer. The night makes a steady hushing sound as it slides past outside the dust-caked window.

"Promise," he repeats.

He looks up and notices his wife's hand dangling down from the upper bunk. He's not sure if she wants to hold his hand, or if she's simply fallen asleep and her arm has slipped limply from her side. She knows his crazy dreams, understands them, and he tries to understand hers. He stares at her hand in the dim light, his eyes large. *Her hand is here, it's now,* he thinks. It's a beautiful hand, the wedding ring he gave her years ago still glistening, her fingers twitching subtly as if they were turning polished shells over and over, or as if they were calling to him. Maybe her fingers are in the middle of a dream, and they're calling him. Acres of shells, acres of green grass. He reaches up to squeeze her hand, and she seems to squeeze back. Every time you give, he thinks, things give back to you. She squeezes his hand and maybe that's all he needs. Maybe, for now, in the darkness, that's enough.

Baseball Hands

My father said a good ballplayer always keeps his glove oiled, and I still remember his advice. After dinner, my son and I sit on the cement front porch steps of our house, oiling our gloves with neat's-foot oil and soft cloths. There's a tenderness about it, this oiling: We oil the joints and hinges of the gloves, the darkened pockets, the intricate web and lacings, the scraped places on the back where we scooped again and again against the dry earth to pull up the sinking line drives. The air fills with the scent of oil, a baseball player's perfume. I glance down, notice that my son has big hands for his age, like mine were when I was young. When we're finished oiling our gloves, our fingers are moist and pliable, too, and we'll smell the fragrant oil on our skin all evening. I slide my hand into the leather, thinking how, with time, the glove becomes one with the hand.

"Why do you have to oil a glove?" my son asks.

"If you oil it enough, you'll play better," I respond automatically.

"But won't you play better if you practice?"

"Well, yeah," I agree with a chuckle. "That too. But if you don't oil a glove, it'll dry out." I recall, as a kid, seeing old gloves in a lost-and-found box in a locker room, their once-golden leather bleached by the dry air to a whitish tan, their skins cracked, brittle, and flaking.

"Oil your glove and you'll always be ready," I add. "That's what Grandpa always used to say."

My son peers into the pocket of his glove. "Ready for what?"

"Ready for anything. Ground ball or line drive. Ready for whatever comes your way."

"Was Grandpa a good ballplayer?"

"Good," I say. "Really good," and suddenly a vision of my father shimmers in front of me. I see him, sitting next to me on the front porch when I was a kid. He's writing, in heavy black letters, our last name on the thick thumb of my baseball glove. He had a compulsion to print our last name on our possessions with a marking pen so nothing would ever get lost. Our name appeared across the thumb of my baseball glove, across the bottoms of my skates, on the edges of the towels we carried to the swimming pool. Our name appeared everywhere, until kids started to make fun of me, saying everything I owned was labeled. But Dad never let us forget who we were. "Even if you lose this," he'd say, "someone'll know it's yours and they'll return it." Then I see him, driving us in the '58 Oldsmobile through the small Midwest towns on his sales job, crossing hand over hand on the steering wheel as we turned a corner. When I was four and five, I'd ride with him on his sales trips, and we'd travel from town to town all day as he made his business contacts. He'd stop at one store after another on a dirt-swirled street with gray corrugated grain elevators. Sometimes I'd go in with him and click pennies in the slots of the vending machines with their multicolored candies held tight by glass bubbles. Other times I'd wait in the car, pressing my small hands to the glass, smudging the window. As the day wore on, and more people said, "No thanks," the skin on Dad's face tightened, erasing his smile. In the evening, we'd return home and he'd be tired, his eyelids drooping as we drove into the flat gray dusk, gravel dust rising behind the car.

"Some day I'm going to do something different," he said once as we drove toward home across the farm fields.

"What do you mean?" I asked. For as long as I'd known my father, he was a salesman.

"Well . . ." He gestured aimlessly with one hand, keeping the other steady on the wheel. "Something else. This job just doesn't fit me."

"What would you do?" I glanced at the road, the blinking white lines rushing toward us.

He paused, contemplated the dust-blown horizon a moment. "I wish I knew," he finally said.

I remember him exhaling a deep breath and glancing down at his old leather briefcase on the car seat between us, the thick black letters of our last name printed in marking pen across the top.

"Dad?" My own son's voice filters through the memory.

"What?" I stare at his nine-year-old face, which suddenly looks older than I remember.

"Did Grandpa ever want to be a major leaguer?" he asks.

"I don't know," I confess. "But he was on a championship amateur team." I recall his stories of the 1936 team, his trip to the city for a two-day tournament.

"Then why didn't he try out for the majors?" he asks.

I shrug.

We sit and talk a few minutes; I tell my son a story—one he's heard before—about the first glove my father bought me. It was a great glove, I explained—so flexible I could catch anything with it. Oil that glove, Dad told me, preserve it. Oil that glove and it will last forever.

"What ever happened to that glove?" my son asks.

"I misplaced it somewhere after high school," I reply. I bought a new glove when I was twenty-six, but even after a few years of playing, it somehow feels awkward and stiff; I still have trouble making those backhanded catches I seemed to make so easily as a kid.

For a moment I stare at my hand in the last sunlight, see the cracks and lines, like a crisscrossed road map. It occurs to me that some people believe you can tell your future just by staring at the hand. They believe they can read your past, predict the events to come. Palm readers stare at the hand, and the hand tells all.

Sometimes I wonder: What will my son become when he grows up? A doctor, a scientist? Will he be like his grandfather, forced to take a lifelong series of odd sales jobs, forced to drive the dulled highways and peddle Nutrena dog food and washing machine parts? Or will he follow his own dreams and aspire to be a pro baseball player? Though he's just turned nine, I know he thinks about playing baseball when he's older.

"Should we go inside?" I ask my son. I tighten the cap on the can of neat's-foot oil.

"No," he responds. "Let's stay out a little longer. Want to play some catch?"

"Sure," I say.

I stand, pick up my glove, and stroll to the middle of the yard. My son follows and we throw a few to each other, the only sound the snapping of the ball in the damp leather pockets.

We play until after sunset, until it's hard to see. My son's arm whips downward as he throws but I can't see the ball until it appears a few feet in front of my face, a dark sphere emerging from the flickering shadows. His enthusiasm grows as he makes quick stabs and jumping catches. When I tell him it's time to quit, he insists on throwing a few more. I narrow my eyes just to see the ball as it flies toward me, and the last throw skims off my glove and rolls, lost beneath the black shadow of the Oldsmobile parked in the drive. I'm about to say *Let it go. We'll find it tomorrow,* but he's already jogging to the car, sliding under it and retrieving the ball.

I sit down on the bottom porch step, and he walks over and lays his glove beside me, the ball tucked safely inside. I glance down and see that his name is not printed anywhere on the glove. For a moment I have a notion to grab a marking pen, write our last name in bold, black letters across the thumb. But I don't. *He'll grow out of this glove,* I think as I study it. *He'll grow out of it soon.*

"You're all set for tomorrow's game," I say. "Grandpa would be proud."

"Yeah." My son nods. "I know—keep your glove oiled and you'll be ready." He lifts one foot to the step and leans his elbow on his thigh. "Think I could ever be a major leaguer?" he asks.

"Only one out of a million kids makes it," I say flatly.

"But what if I'm that one?"

I give him a half-smile but don't answer. I lean back against the hard cement step and ponder the evening sky, the patterns of light and darkness, the red layer still coating the horizon. I want to tell him that it's just a dream so many of us share when we grow up, until the real world, with all its practicality, hits us in the face like a line drive. When we're seventeen or eighteen, we wake one morning, and know it will never happen. I want to tell him that, as we get older, we all go through this: these cycles of yearning and loss, these dreams that ripen, then dry up and turn brittle. I want to tell him, but instead I remain silent. We live our lives as best we can, and we keep our gloves oiled just in case. We keep our gloves oiled, thinking maybe they'll catch the ball better than *we* ever could. My son slides next to me on the front porch. Before we go in, we sit there a moment, staring at the horizon, gently sliding our gloves on and off our hands.

Lights: Joe and Marilyn, an American Love Story

The first time she saw him was on that earthen diamond—she watched his loping strides, smooth as a liquid
spilled from a glass on a bright green countertop. He skimmed
the ball from center field and, with a decisive motion of arm
and shoulder, threw it home. She heard the crowds cheer him
as he hit a line drive twice as far as the skinny boys back in
Texas ever hit one, and as she watched him circle the bases, she
knew she was in love.

What she needed was a man like that, she thought, a man
who slicks his hair back with water, a man in a pinstriped
Yankee uniform who could lift her with his wide forearms,
carry her away from herself and all her mirrors. She pictured
him setting her down in the entryway of a small white cottage, the sunlight glistening off its sugary shutters. The door
would lock out the past. Inside, behind white lace curtains,
they could drink each other as if they were elixirs. She
wouldn't need to part her bright red lips and tilt her head to
one side in her imitation of seductiveness; she didn't have to
smile if she didn't want to. She could stand in front of him as
herself, just herself. Then, if she wanted to, she'd slide the
strap of her dress off one milky shoulder and Joe would be
her camera, the only camera she needed.

* * *

The war had ended a few years before, in '45. Now America was a winner, and the whole country wanted to cheer. Joe stepped to the plate and swung the bat, and each time he did, he killed Hitler. Each time he swung, another fleet of GIs swept onto the beach at Normandy. Each time he swung, another factory opened its doors, the kitchen stoves and auto parts rushing down the assembly line too fast to count. Ah, it was great then, after the war. Nothing could stop us from growing. Everyone wanted to shout and throw confetti and sit under a Yankee sky in a stadium where this new gangly kid could hit the ball all the way to the year 2000.

After one game, outside the entrance of the stadium, he stood, a little uncomfortable in his baggy suit. Something glistened in the corner of his eye. Then he turned and saw her, her face like a diamond caught in the sun. He saw her, one creamy shoulder exposed, as she glided up slowly to him, parting the bobbing reporters like a sea. "Mr. DiMaggio," she gasped, "may I have your autograph?" Joe doesn't remember if he smiled, or muttered a word from his shy mouth, or just looked at her. All he knows is that he pulled out a pen, clicked it, then almost forgot what she'd asked him. When he signed his autograph, it was as if his signature was drawing a blue swirling line that connected his heart straight to Marilyn's.

Cameras from everywhere surrounded the wedding ceremony: The bulbs waited to flash, and all of America was watching. It was a winning concoction: the queen and the athlete, beauty and skill, the breathy sex goddess and the shy young man, Hollywood and New York. The press mixed it up and watched it bubble and splashed it across the front page of all the newspapers the next morning. America wanted to believe, and we drank it all in.

* * *

The next morning, Joe looked into Marilyn's eyes, saw their fiery softness, and Marilyn looked into Joe's and knew he could see all the way beneath her skin.

America imagined that, on their honeymoon, they stayed awake all night in a small cottage. They toasted each other with champagne, and their wakefulness was a cloud they both drifted on, a cloud floating high across the country. Joe noticed how clear her skin was, how glowing, almost like light itself. So much beauty, so much sheer beauty he'd never seen in his life. The simple act of lying next to her might make anyone feel clumsy and imperfect. He slid his hands around her and held her carefully, like some fragile glass rose he knew might break at his touch.

And she saw Joe, and knew he was the body of all good men, men who were kind and sweet, men she'd searched for her whole life. He never leered at her like they did; he covered her with his strong arms and somehow calmed those turbulent winds that always seemed to be circling inside her mind.

In one smooth motion they leaned forward to kiss, and in one smooth motion they pulled away and nine months had passed and they saw they were far apart. She, back in Hollywood beneath bright lights that could blister a pale cheek, he, strolling the fringes of an empty Yankee Stadium, picturing himself still running for a ball, a meteorite slicing the air in front of him.

When the marriage ended, America woke up suddenly and didn't know where it was: The news couldn't be true, everyone thought—their sweethearts were breaking up. When the marriage ended, the flashbulbs exploded in Joe's and Marilyn's faces, burning their eyes, making both of them see spots in their vision for weeks as they woke alone. When the marriage ended, America woke up and saw that something had changed. Maybe the storybook's final pages were torn out, the edges suddenly jagged and rough. Maybe the world wasn't all Victory and love and sweethearts and smiles. For the first time America realized that maybe not everything was going to last, maybe there'd be losses that no one expected.

Marilyn opened the bottle, poured the contents into her palm. She gazed at them: The pills might have been a handful of diamonds, or candy. She dropped the first one onto her tongue. She tasted it, savored its sweet bitterness. Then she swallowed it with a toast of water. *Pure water,* she thought for a fleeting moment. *That's the only thing to drink. It's cleansing. It keeps the skin clear.* She took the pills one by one until she finished them all. She drained the tall glass slowly, felt all of Niagara Falls pouring into her, a thousand honeymooners watching from the shore. *Pure,* she thought. Then she leaned back and felt a kind of glow on the back of her head as her hair spread into a corona on the white satin pillow. Who knows if she had brief dreams of Joe that evening, of Joe's smiling face leaning over her, saying he was sorry. What's certain is that she saw a camera gliding nearer and nearer to her for a cover-girl closeup, the bright lights, numbing lights, like the floodlights of a baseball field, moving in closer, closer, the light searing through her blue eyes, and then she smiled for the camera as all that beautiful brightness enveloped her.

When Marilyn died, Joe felt a part of himself die: The grassy fields inside him withered. Eyes hidden by sunglasses, Joe went through the motions, making the funeral arrange-

ments. Joe saw to it that no one from Hollywood was allowed to attend the funeral. He believed, as he stood close to
the coffin, his dark suit wrinkled, that it wasn't a suicide. Not
a suicide at all. It was Hollywood that destroyed her.

After the funeral, he went into seclusion for months. The
press stood outside his door waiting, but Joe wouldn't utter
a sentence about the marriage or Marilyn, his sorrow too
deep, too painful for words. Each year after that, Joe,
wrapped in a trench coat, placed roses at Marilyn's gravesite
on her birthday.

Years later, Joe shows up on television, selling coffeemak-
ers for Mr. Coffee. His hair is washed gray, and he's lost
weight, and young kids look up at their sets and ask their
parents, "Who's that?" Their parents might answer, or they
might just go silent in a kind of awe, not hearing their child's
question. They might just nod at Joe in his gray suit on the
screen and reminisce about America's sweethearts for a few
seconds. Then they might feel a sudden urge for a cup of
coffee to keep them awake that evening.

Before the filming of a new commercial, Joe sits in his small
dressing room somewhere in Hollywood. He wraps his big
hand around the coffee cup on the desk. He's alone now, so
alone he can almost taste it. He can taste his middle age—a
flavor he can't quite identify. The lights around the set are
darkened. They remind him of the lights over Yankee Stadium when he retired and left the field for the last time: cold,
unblinking. Drowsy, he rests his elbows on the veneer and
dozes a moment. Who knows if he has brief dreams of Marilyn that afternoon, of the warm oval of her face leaning over
him. "Sorry," she might be whispering. "Sorry."

A knock on the door, reminding him of the next shoot, startles him. Though he doesn't notice, the sleeve of his suit jacket soaks up his spilled coffee as if it were dying of thirst. He rubs his temples, trying to clear his mind: The losses are too much, too huge to even think back on.

On the set, he seems self-conscious as he faces the lights, bright as the future. They seem to be staring at him, waiting for him to act. The director hands him a plastic cup; Joe sees the coffee evaporating as the steam rises in wisps. And though there's no audience except for a handful of crew members, Joe smiles into the cool glass of the camera lens. Who knows what he might be thinking as he looks into the camera— maybe he's trying to imagine the millions of Americans who used to cheer him. "That's it, Joe," the director coaxes in a bored voice. "This one's a winner. This one's a home run." The camera glides toward him; America is always watching close-up. Joe lifts a toast toward the viewers, swirls the cup gently and glances into it, but can't tell if the dark liquid is moving or not.

Ancient Fires

The clouded sky above the town ripples like dented aluminum as the father and his teenage son stand at opposite corners of a vacant lot.

"You ready?" the father asks as he cocks his arm to throw a baseball.

"I s'pose." The son shrugs, tapping his new glove on the side of his leg.

"Better be," the father says as he leans into a throw, " 'cause it's coming at you."

The son drops the throw, picks the ball up, scowls at it, then tosses it back. The father's next throw skips off the thumb of the son's glove, bounds several yards to his left, and thumps against the old shed in the back corner of the lot. The son glares at his father. "Not so hard," he calls.

"Come on," his dad chides, shaking his head. "You should be able to catch those."

Sometimes the father sits in his living room on his La-Z-Boy chair, looks up from his *Reader's Digest,* and wonders about his son—how he's seemed to change these past few months. *I don't know why I ever bought him that glove,* the father thinks, *the way he takes care of it. I should've given it to a nephew, or even saved it for myself, in case I start playing ball again. I keep finding it all over the place—in the basement, on the front porch, in the back hall. Damn thing was expensive, too. A Rawlings. The kind like they use in the majors. Cost me nearly a hundred dollars. I remember standing in that hardware store, thumbing through my wallet to make sure I had enough to cover it. Maybe I shouldn't have gotten him a present in the first place. Maybe the kid's getting too old for presents.*

The father draws a slow breath into his barrel chest, gazes toward his baseball trophies that glimmer on the shelf above the TV. *All I want is for him to play like I know he can play,* he thinks. *That's all. It's that simple. Just be as good as he can, and work at it the way I did in high school. I know his best effort would carry him a lot farther than mine carried me.* He releases his breath gradually, his chest deflating like an inner tube losing air. *I almost hate to admit he's got more talent than I ever had as a ballplayer. But I can't tell him that. He's always putting me off, the way he sits in his room with the lights out and stares at the ceiling. And when we eat dinner, he looks down at his plate and doesn't say a word. Like he's ten thousand years away or something. He never says anything lately, except to talk about some* Star Wars *pinball machine, about who got a million points in one game, who got a replay. Here his mother and I sit, worrying about him, and he spends hours playing pinball. I just don't know what to say. But I do know one thing. I should have never bought him that glove. One of these days, when we head out to play catch, I'm going to grab that new glove from the closet, and when he reaches for it, I'll pull it back from him. He'll look at me, confused, so I'll say, "Use your old glove," and toss him that little mitt he used when he was a kid. Then I'll slip on the new glove and just tell him, "This one's mine.*

This one's mine now." And that would say all I need to say.
That would be that.

I never asked for a new glove, the son thinks as he crosses
the high school parking lot to his car after baseball practice.
My old one worked fine.

It bothers him that, without asking him, his father just
stopped one day and bought the glove for him. *What's he
trying to do, anyway,* he wonders, *make me into a pro or
something?*

His dad avidly follows the high school team. He sits with
the other fathers in the front row of the bleachers, and sometimes they smoke thin cigars and sip cans of Blatz beer or half
pints of liquor from paper bags. *They're loyal to this crummy
town,* the son thinks as he glances at them from the bench,
they actually like *this place.* After close plays, his dad's low-
pitched voice growls at the umpire: "Are you an idiot, ump,
or just a Neanderthal?" The son hears the men laughing at
the comment. Sometimes, after the game, some of his dad's
white-shirted, beer-bellied pals waddle near the bench. "Do
you know how good your old man was?" they ask the son
proudly, their words floating on a thick scent of liquor. "His
records'll last forever." The boy just shrugs indifferently. One
of them pats him on the back and says: " 'Bout time you tried
out for the majors, ain't it? That new glove'll sure come in
handy."

Each day after baseball practice, the son drinks cherry
Cokes and plays pinball at the soda fountain with his buddies. He could stare for a long time at that brightly colored
machine, the shiny steel ball bouncing off the quick flippers,
the targets binging and flashing each time you hit them. *As
long as you don't tilt it,* he thinks as he plays, *the game could*

go for hours. After pinball, the son and his buddies sit on the park bench, their backs to the statue of the Civil War soldier, and light up the Kool cigarettes they've hidden at the bottoms of their duffels. Once his buddies chuckled as he dropped the lit stub of his cigarette into the bronze barrel of the soldier's rifle. *So much for heroes,* he scoffed.

Each day he drives home past the tarnished tin-roofed houses of the town, the rows and rows of them, each one just the same as the next, with their sagging porches held up by paint-chipped pillars. *These dumps would never last in a twister,* he thinks. *This whole town would be leveled.* Some days he tries to count the dingy houses as he passes, but he always loses count by the time he reaches the stop sign on Main. He's never told his father, but he can't wait until he can leave this place, spin out from his gravel driveway and watch his father and the houses and the crumbling brick facades of the downtown shrink to nothing in the rearview mirror. *I'm no star,* he often thinks. *I'm just a kid with a glove I'm not used to. I'm just a second-string junior on a high school team.*

The son strolls toward the shed to pick up the throw he just missed.

On the other side of the lot, the father notices how slowly his son covers the thirty yards. *It'll take him all year to get there,* he thinks. He notices how the boy carries the new glove loosely on his hand, like he's just about to drop it.

The scene from last week replays in the father's mind, and the memory makes him angry all over again. He found the glove lying in the dirt of the backyard like some abandoned toy. He knelt down, picked it up as if it were a small, stray, injured animal. He brought it into the house and oiled it, shaking his head. *Damn kid,* he thought. *I have to take care of his damn glove for him.*

That day, when the son came home, laughing on the front sidewalk with his buddies, the father was waiting on the screened porch, staring through the gray mesh of the door, his arms crossed stiffly in front of his chest. He thought he noticed the faint smell of smoke on the boys.

"You left this out in the yard," the father blurted, interrupting their talk. He held the glove next to his face.

The boys went silent and his son just stared at him blankly. "No I didn't," he replied.

"Then how the hell did it get there?" the father asked, his voice grating against the walls of the porch like sandpaper.

"I wouldn't know." The son shrugged. Without another word, he slipped past his father, let the door clack shut behind him.

The son picks up the ball; a red mark scars the leather where it glanced off the shed's painted wall. He studies the ball's scuff marks as though trying to read them like some strange hieroglyphic. He turns and flings the ball back to his father. It's a bad throw, off to one side.

The father reaches agilely to his left and snags the ball. His mouth curves into a tight-lipped smile; he knows he still has the ballplaying instincts he had years ago when he was named all-conference high school shortstop and led the league in batting and fielding.

The son doesn't acknowledge the smile; instead, he pushes his fist into the stiff webbing of the glove, trying to shape it. His father keeps reminding him how much the glove cost, and he hates that. "Don't leave it on the porch," his dad warned the day he gave it to him. "Could get stolen. Keep it inside."

The glove works okay, but the son's just not used to it yet. He doesn't like the way it feels too big for his hand, feels like it could slip off his fingers if he jabbed it in the air for a high line drive.

After a few more throws, the son drops another one. Disgusted, he slams the glove down to the ground.

"Damn it all," the father shouts, "don't throw your glove. A ballplayer never throws his glove." He has a notion to walk over, pick up the glove, carry it straight back to the house. And that would be that.

"Let's quit." The son spits out the words. "I don't wanna play anymore."

The father has an urge to shout at his son, to tell him everything that makes him so damn mad lately, but then he thinks better of it. He keeps it inside.

Instead, he speaks in a controlled voice, a hoarse whisper, almost. "We're not quitting," he says, his back going rigid as if his spine were filling with iron. "We're not quitting yet."

The son paces around the glove, sulking. He focuses on the bare spots in the grass. *I'm never good enough for him,* he thinks, *never.* His gaze shifts back to the glove, and he feels all the anger circling like a whirlwind inside his body. *Maybe he'd catch better with this thing. Maybe he's the one who should be wearing it.*

"You've got to get in front of the damn ball," the father says, half coaching his son, half chiding.

"I *was* in front of it," the son says defensively, lifting his arms into the air.

"Aw, come on," says the father, shaking his head side to side with a throaty, sarcastic chuckle. "You just stabbed at it. Don't be lazy."

The son tips his face toward the low hanging layer of gray clouds. He hates these words, words he's heard a thousand times before. *Don't be lazy. Put a little effort into it, will you?*

The father stares beyond his son to the abandoned shed, its padlocked door, its boarded windows that serve no purpose, the red flecks of paint chipping off the weathered wood onto the untrimmed grass. *Damn thing's going to fall over some day,* he thinks. *Nothing lasts that many years.* He focuses back on his son, his lazy son. "Come on," he commands. "We're gonna play 'til you get this thing right."

"Jeez," the son mutters. "It's just a game."

"No it's not," his father replies.

The boy finally picks up the glove and the baseball. He stands there, looking at the shed and the run-down houses that surround the lot, and for a moment it seems like they're all leaning toward him, it seems like the whole sky is leaning toward him. He thinks of the steel ball after he tilts the pinball machine: The lights blink out and the machine goes silent beneath the layer of glass, and all he can hear is the whirring of the ball as it rolls toward the immovable flippers.

The son looks back at his father's silhouette: It's flat, as though he's cut from sheet metal, like a tin target in a shooting gallery at the county fair.

The father lifts his old glove into the air in front of his face. "Right here," he says coolly, his chin tipped backward slightly. "Right now."

The boy's cheeks flush scarlet. He rears back and throws one as hard as he can. The father doesn't have to move his glove a fraction of an inch as the baseball slaps hard in the pocket.

The father whips the ball back to his son on a line. The quickness of the throw startles the son, but he stops the ball directly in front of his chin. The sting radiates outward to his fingertips. He takes a step forward, fires the ball at his father.

The father gloves it, takes a step forward, and returns the ball with a grunt and a sweep of his arm.

Without a word, they stalk closer and closer with each throw, their jaws tightening. They hunch toward each other until they're only ten feet apart, both of them panting for air as they whip fastballs at each other. The ball punches the pockets of their gloves; their palms burn like ancient fires.

"Now you're talking," the father says through his clenched teeth that, from the houses down the street, might look like a grin. "That's it. That's it. Now you're talking."

What About the World

He'll tell you his name's Darwin, and though he's been out of school a long time, he likes to play baseball alone on his old high school field. He likes to stand across from the brick building and drive the ball toward the wall with the crumbling cement between the large stones. Each day he jogs to the field with a duffel bag and a chipped baseball bat and hits fly balls toward that stone wall that will probably be there a million years. Some of his friends his age say *You can't just play baseball all the time. You gotta do other things, too.* His relatives say *Aren't you getting a little old for that?* He never knows how to reply. He just grins at them. Grins. There's no way in the world he can agree with them, no way.

His wife, Eileen, keeps telling him there's a lot more to life than baseball. Some evenings, when she's reading the newspaper, she sees him studying the box scores or relacing his glove, and she looks up at him intently. She tells him there's poverty and there's fighting in the streets. He knows that. He knows there's a lot more going on, but Jesus, he thinks, what can you do about it?

"I know you love baseball," she says, "and that's okay. But shouldn't you think more about the rest of the world?"

His answer's a shrug. He has no comeback for that question, a question that's grown too large for him over the years.

He and his wife don't disagree much, but on the subject of baseball, once in a while they disagree. Sometimes, when he grabs his frayed duffel bag and slips out the door, he notices her tensed facial muscles, her soft cheeks seeming to pull inward. Returning from the field an hour later with sweat like honey beading his forehead, he sees that her lips still draw a taut line. But later at night, they always touch each other, lying as close to each other as they possibly can. Her breath on his shoulder is pure and sweet as a breeze blowing across a new-mown outfield. Sometimes, Darwin thinks, they both fear what's out there.

It's a kind of urgency that makes him leave each afternoon for the field. He loves to be alone out there, just for a while. He loves to toss that baseball softly in front of his face, watch it balance there on the air like a small white leather planet before he hits it.

He reminds himself that he's not a kid, not a kid at all. In fact, he'd never admit it to anyone, but the thought has occurred to him that he just might be getting a little too old for this game. He knows he's not immune, immune to the gravity and the wind, knows no one is. The whiskers on his chin look gray at the tips when he doesn't shave for a couple of days. He knows that. And his eyes are getting worse lately; when he tries to spot a ball flying in the distance, he has to narrow his eyes to see it. Sometimes the ball shrinks to a dust speck and then disappears and he has no idea where it'll land.

But he doesn't care about that. He doesn't *feel* too old, he tells Eileen, and that's what counts. So he's a businessman in town, he thinks, so what? When he walks on a ball field, dressed in shorts, a torn T-shirt, and his scuffed-up tennies, he feels transformed, as if that succulent grass beneath his old shoes were youth itself, sending its power up through his limping legs.

"What about a child?" Eileen asks. She's brought up the subject of adopting a baby before, yet, for some reason he doesn't understand, he keeps putting the discussion off.

She hands him the flier from the adoption agency. On its cover is a black-and-white photo of a malnourished child. The child stares at him and the stare hurts. Darwin stares back, and he knows he has to make up his mind. "You'd be a great father." Her voice softens.

"What do you think, Darwin?" Eileen says. "You'd be a great father." Her voice softens.

"Think so?"

"Of course I do." She slides her arms around his waist and smiles at him. She leans and kisses him on the cheek and he can smell the scent of her perfume, like the lilacs around the edge of the ball field.

"We should put our name in at the agency," says Darwin. He realizes it's getting a little late for their first child.

"Okay," she says, anticipation in her voice. "How about tomorrow?"

"No, not tomorrow. I can't tomorrow."

She inhales a slow breath. "How long can we wait?" she asks.

When he doesn't answer, she pulls her arms from his waist and turns away.

How long can we wait? After she leaves the room, the words scrape in Darwin's mind like dried leaves circling in the wind. For a while, as he sits alone in the living room, he feels the world outside, pressing on all the windows of the house.

*   *   *

Sometimes Darwin thinks about the headlight incident that happened last month. He has never told Eileen about it. He was hitting baseballs at the far end of the high school field, and that day, one of his longer hits bounced on the sidewalk and into the street beyond the corner of the school. He heard a thump, followed by a high-pitched clinking.

In a few seconds, a car pulled around the corner and parked at the curb where Darwin was batting. A broad-faced, heavyset man slid out of the car. He waddled toward the field in a blue suit and tie, holding Darwin's baseball. The man walked up close, shook the ball in front of his face. Darwin could see a pale gash in the brown leather ball.

"This your ball, sir?" the man asked, puffing out the words.

Darwin hated it when people called him *sir.* "Guess so," Darwin finally said, admitting his guilt.

"Well, you hit my headlight with it," the man said, pointing with his other hand back toward his car. His expression was like a watch spring coiled tight. "That's a brand new car," he added. The words sounded thick and round as they came out of his mouth.

"Sorry," said Darwin, "real sorry." He held out his hand for the ball. The man lowered it into Darwin's palm.

"Sorry won't do it. You know that's a halogen headlight. It'll cost me at least fifteen bucks to fix it." The man's left cheek twitched.

Darwin looked at the car, parked by the curb, its one eye a bare socket, blinded. He reached into his pocket, handed the man fifteen.

"You're lucky," the man said, stuffing the bills into his polyester suit pants stretched tightly across his hips.

Darwin looked puzzled.

"Lucky all you hit was the headlight," said the man. "You could've hit the windshield or the fender or something. That's a brand new car, you know."

"How much does a car like that cost?" asked Darwin.

"Twenty-five grand," the man said proudly.

"Sheez," exclaimed Darwin.

The man glanced toward the far side of the field. "You hit that ball from way back there?" he asked.

"Sure," said Darwin.

The man shook his head from side to side. "Pretty good shot," he said as he turned to walk back to his car.

"Just lucky," said Darwin.

Today, as Darwin jogs to the baseball field alone, the voice inside his head speaks to him again. *How long can you keep doing this?* the voice wants to know. *Men your age take up golf. Baseball's too fast, too dangerous. How long can you keep going?*

Forever, he wants to answer. *Forever.* Instead he mutters aloud, "I don't know."

But what about the fighting? the voice asks. *What about the wars?*

Darwin hates it when the voice talks to him. Why do his thoughts always seem to intrude?

What about the wars? the voice insists.

What about them? Darwin thinks. There are no wars here. I'm just playing ball.

Playing. The voice spits out the word as though it tasted sour.

I just go to a field and hit a ball and then chase it, Darwin thinks. There's no victory here, no defeat. It's great.

He jogs to his favorite spot on the field, his favorite spot in the world, drops his duffel bag filled with scuffed baseballs. Somewhere in his head, he hears the voice speaking again. *What about world hunger?* it says.

I'm feeding the hunger, Darwin thinks as he tosses a ball into the air and swings hard.

Eileen still seems angry at him during dinner. She eats without speaking, her fork clicking hard on the china plate.

Later, before he falls asleep, he thinks about it. *It does feed me, doesn't it?* he thinks. *When I walk away from that field after a couple hours of baseball, I'm a better person. I can face the world. I can care for people, and give them a smile. I don't need to compete with them, because I feel better about myself.* He sees himself hitting a line drive that ricochets off the big wall, knocking a triangle of cement loose. *I'm stopping the wars right here,* he thinks. *I'm stopping them inside myself. I'm playing ball, and I'm stopping death, right there on that little sandlot field.*

"Dar," his wife says.

"Yes?" He rolls off the pillow, sits up.

"I still love you. You know that, don't you?"

He props himself on one elbow. "What do you mean, *still?* You make it sound like it could change."

"Everything can change," she says, "can't it?" She sighs and closes her eyes. "Sometimes I think about the future," she says, her voice sounding hollow. "It's out there, waiting for us, but we don't know what it's going to be. Sometimes," she says, her words catching a little in her throat, "sometimes I try to imagine it. To see it, almost. But I just can't tell what it is."

That night Darwin dreams he's sitting at the dining room table, staring at the photograph of the homeless, hungry child on the front of the flier. He stares into the caves of the child's dark, hollow eyes. Suddenly the child climbs out of the photograph and stands in front of him in his living room. As if it were being pumped with air, healthy flesh fills out the child's slight frame. The child smiles. Darwin looks lovingly at the child's eyes and the child gazes back at him. Then the child reaches out one hand, and when Darwin touches it, the child shrivels, becomes flat and thin again, and shrinks back into the black-and-white photograph on the table.

Darwin wakes in the middle of the night and slips quietly down the stairs. He sees the flier, illuminated by the moonlight that filters through the custom bay windows. He stares at the photograph of the homeless child, stares at it a long time. But the child doesn't climb out of the photograph. It doesn't move at all, just stares back at him.

At breakfast the next morning, Eileen does a kind of dance of avoidance when she's near him. When he steps into the bathroom to wash his hands, she slides her makeup into her purse and walks out. When he leans toward her to pour her coffee, she turns her face toward the cabinets. Tired of the silence, Darwin sets down his glass of milk, walks over to Eileen, who stands where the low sun shines through the narrow slat blinds, cutting the dining room with layers of light. He puts his hands on her shoulders, turns her toward him.

She pulls back and stares into his green eyes. "Do you care about me?" she says.

"Of course I do," he says. Then he adds, "I'm lucky to have you."

"I wonder sometimes."

"You're my designated hitter," he says. "You're my manager. You're the only one who can bunt me home with a sacrifice."

"Darwin," she says, "stop talking baseball to me."

He lifts his open palms toward the white ceiling with a boyish grin. "It's the only language I know."

"Come on, Darwin." The angry tone of her voice erases his grin. "This isn't a game. I'm serious now. What about us? What about our family?"

He sits down on the straight-backed wooden chair. "What do you mean, *family?*"

"A family is a man and a woman. And a child. A *child.* We've got love to share. So we've got to think about it. We've got to decide. No," she corrects herself, "*you've* got to decide. Soon."

He stands there, unable to answer. As usual, he feels like a baserunner caught halfway between third and home, uncertain which way to sprint.

Later that day, after work, Darwin lifts his duffel bag full of baseballs and turns toward the door.

"I'm going out," he says tentatively to Eileen, who sits on the love seat reading some folders from the Family Crisis Center where she works.

"But Darwin, what about . . ." Eileen's voice trails off.

"What about what?" he asks, though he thinks he knows the rest of her question.

"Nothing," she says. "Go ahead." There's a certain indifference in her voice that he can't interpret. She sets down the folder and doesn't look at him, just sort of gazes off into the still air of the living room. It's like there's a pane of Plexiglas between them these past couple of days, and he couldn't reach through it if he tried.

For a moment he just stands motionless in the front door-way. As if he wanted another response from her, he mutters, "I've just got to play a little ball."

She sighs. A few long seconds go by. "I know," she finally says.

As he steps off the front porch, he hears the voice inside his head again. *What about the world?* it asks. This time it's louder than he's ever heard it, and more demanding. The voice is crisp and metallic, like a clock ticking. *What about it?*

I'll answer that question, Darwin thinks, as soon as I get back.

He jogs to the field and hits a few baseballs that roll to the ten-foot stone wall and slap off its surface. He stares at the wall, its cement waiting to crumble. Stares at it, knowing he's never hit one over it from this far back. Then he tosses the ball above his head, and his muscles surprise the quiet air. He hits a drive farther than he's hit one all season. Farther than he's ever hit one in his life. It clears the wall and disappears.

On the way home, he thinks of the adoption application. He'll talk to Eileen as soon as he gets back. He'll tell her about how he's made up his mind, that they'll fill out the application tonight, then toast it with champagne. He'd like to adopt a needy child from Colombia or Ecuador or Peru. "What about it?" he'll say, his smile making a sound like a round of applause.

Reaching his front sidewalk, he feels younger than he has for years; his muscles tingle, and he springs up the front step with a motion smooth as love. *You and me,* he plans to tell her. *You and me. The two of us are the world.* He jogs upstairs, calling her name. The sound echoes off the plaster hallway.

In the second-story bedroom he finds the closet door open, her clothes gone, a black tangle of hangers on the floor. He stands in the middle of the room, a room that seems, all of a sudden, too large. He catches a glimpse of his face in the dresser mirror: the rivulets of sweat, the matted, receding hairline, the eyes in their sockets that suddenly look so hungry and so scared.

He lifts the shade and stands in front of the window, sees the panes separated by wood, the concentric swirls of the fine, varnished grain. For the first time, he notices a hairline crack across the glass of one pane. He traces it with his finger. Then he narrows his eyes and stares beyond it, stares out past the yard, past the ball field, to the narrow county road that points into the hazy distance. He just stands there and looks out as if he could, from that height, see the whole world.

Baseball, Fathers, and Dreams

Summer 1959

The beauty of it is that I'm eight years old, and I'm sitting in the upper-deck grandstand of Milwaukee County Stadium with my father at my first big-league baseball game. The excitement's so thick I can taste it, like the ice cream bar Dad will buy me later in the game. It's still the first inning, Warren Spahn winds up to pitch to Willie Mays, and I lean forward intently. As Spahn delivers, Mays swings and hits a foul ball that rises and arcs through the floodlights, white and spinning and right toward us. Everyone in our section jumps to their feet, arms dancing to greet the ball. The baseball skips off the hands of one set of fans, bounces off a second set of fingers, then lands with a thump in the back of my chair and nestles there. I reach down quickly and grab the ball, hold it high in the air like my first caught fish as my father pats me on the back and beams.

Before the game, as we walked through the parking lot to the stadium, I said to my dad: "Maybe I'll get a baseball." I looked up anxiously at the high side of the stadium.

"That's not very likely," my father said.

"Why not?" I ask.

"Do you know what the chances are?" he said. "It hardly happens in a lifetime. I've been to games for years and never even got *near* a baseball."

My answer was a pop of my fist in the palm of my glove as we walked up the stadium ramp.

By the seventh inning, the game was tied—Braves 2, Giants 2—but my dad, always the practical one, wanted to leave the game early.

"To avoid the traffic jam in the lot," he told me. I really wanted to stay for the rest of the game, but I stood up dutifully to leave, craning my neck to see a last bit of the game through the steel rafters as we walked down the zigzagging cement ramps. When we reached the parking lot, I saw a ball rise and fall in the floodlights, could hear the low-pitched collective groan of the fans as Willie McCovey hit a three-run homer.

After the game, about ten-thirty that night, Dad drove us through dark and deserted downtown Milwaukee streets, pulled over in front of a White Castle. The restaurant was dwarfed by tall downtown buildings, and its neon-rimmed picture window tossed a bright yellow square onto the sidewalk. A bell on the door jingled us into the smoky room, where a man, his stained apron clinging to his stomach, his paper cap pulled low on his forehead, hunched over the counter while Dad and I, the only customers, read the grease-mapped menus and ordered.

"Braves lost it tonight, eh?" the man muttered.

"Yeah," said Dad. "But the boy got a ball."

I proudly held up my souvenir and grinned.

The man squinted at it. "Nice one," he said. "Who from?"

"Mays," Dad said.

The man nodded in approval, and turned to the back of the counter. The french fries sizzled a moment—the only sound in the place—then our order clinked in front of us on thick china plates.

I remember sitting there that night on the red vinyl stool and eating the hamburger, which seemed to taste better than anything I'd ever eaten. My father and I didn't say anything, just sat at the counter, surrounded by a halo of smoke inside that shell of light, our elbows propped on the whorled Formica. I held that new baseball, turning it over and over in my fingers. Sometimes I believe we're still sitting there. It's as if we're held there, timeless, like an Edward Hopper painting, for thirty years.

1988

On a warm June morning when the sky was a hazy yellow from the smoke of distant forest fires, my father died of a heart attack. Our family was shocked; he'd been in good health for years.

That morning he died, I was three hundred miles away on a field, playing baseball with a few friends. That morning he died, I hit a high line drive toward the red wood-slat fence in left. It was my best hit of the day, and it looked like the ball would carry over the fence, but it lost momentum in the air and struck the fence, snapping one of the wood slats with a clack. I didn't hear about my father until I came back to the house and walked into the kitchen. When the phone rang on the wall, I was standing there—winded, sweating, carrying a brown frayed baseball in my hand.

Summer 1989

My eight-year-old son and I walk into the Metrodome for a Minnesota Twins game on a Sunday in April. We hurry past the gates until we get to the left-field bleachers, then rush down the aisle.

"Here," my son says as he intuitively selects a spot a few seats up from the fence.

"What about over there?" I ask, pointing a few rows up. "Those seats look good."

"No," he insists. "Right here."

He seems so certain that I don't move an inch. We sit on top of the seats in anticipation.

Before the game, my son had said: "Let's get there early for batting practice. Maybe we'll get a baseball."

"Don't count on it," I said. In that instant, my father's voice echoed inside my head.

As the Twins begin batting practice, Kirby Puckett steps to the plate, swings, and we can hear the bat connect with the ball—the sharp crack echoes back and forth in the dome.

The ball's hit deep, and straight at us.

"Look," I call to my son, feeling the adrenaline push out my words. "Here it comes."

I watch the ball rise in a smooth arc, then fall toward us from the white pillow roof of the Metrodome. The baseball bounds off the seats two rows ahead of us, bounds again, then skips into the front row where no one's sitting. Before I realize it, we're climbing headlong over the blue seats, tripping and thumping our way toward the front.

When we reach the front row, time thickens as we move in slow motion through the glue of air. Suddenly my son breaks the spell by lifting the ball, holding it high above his head.

*   *   *

Afterward, my son and I pull into a McDonald's for burgers. My son carries the baseball through the restaurant, cradling it in his hands as though it were a fragile crystal ball. As we eat, he turns his souvenir over and over.

We sit there a few minutes, and I tell him about stopping for hamburgers with my father that night, years ago, after the Braves game. Tell him about the man in the white paper hat and the island of light and how I felt like we were the only two people on earth. Tell him how fathers always leave the game too early.

That night I dream again and again of sitting in those bleachers, seeing Kirby's bat whip around, hearing the echoing *crackackack* as the ball finds the center of the wood bat. I dream again and again of the ball leaping into the air, straight at us, dream of it falling in its slow-motion arc. When it lands, I grab it, and suddenly I'm eight years old in Milwaukee County Stadium again, sitting next to my father, who grins broadly as I hold up Willie Mays's baseball.

During an All-Star Game, I saw a pregame feature on Kirby Puckett, who stood in front of his open locker in the clubhouse. Taped to the locker door was a photograph of Kirby's idol: Willie Mays.

Suddenly it occurred to me—Willie and Kirby both play center field gracefully, both are great hitters, both are All-Stars, both made famous catches in World Series games. Maybe it's all just coincidence, the connections between my son and me, between Willie and Kirby, who wasn't even born the day Mays hit that foul ball to me in Milwaukee. But the more I think about it, the more I believe it has something to do with the way time twists itself in cycles. Years pass, and you see yourself change and stay the same. Maybe it's a little like running the bases as you try for an inside-the-park homer: You begin at home, and you run a frantic, panting circuit past first, around second, toward third, and—if you're lucky—you end up at home again.

The Future

I can imagine a time when I'm just a memory in my grown son's mind. My son will take his young son to a ball game somewhere in a stadium that hasn't even been built. My son will tell the boy about his baseball souvenir from Kirby Puckett years before. He'll tell him stories about his father and his grandfather at a Milwaukee Braves game way back in the fifties.

Then he'll lean close, look into his son's eyes, and tell him the sad truth: Fathers always leave the game too early.

The two of them will walk into the stadium, and, guided by his son's small hand, they'll sit in the right spot and turn their faces toward home. Then a batter, a young star who's not even born yet, will swing hard at the ball, and hit it just right, as he was destined to, and the ball will rise from his bat, high and clean and arcing, and my son will know. He'll know that the world changes, but there are a few constants: baseball, fathers, dreams. His eight-year-old son won't understand; all he'll know is that a new, glowing baseball drops toward him like an egg as the sky gives birth. The beauty of it is that he won't understand it yet. But he will. Just give him time.

FIVE

The Endless
Sprint Toward
Home

The Language of
Baseball Caps

One February evening, when my best friend from high school called me long distance about getting together for our class reunion, he told me that he thought he could still find his high school baseball cap in a box in his garage. As he talked, I tried to picture his old ball cap, back there among the taped, splintered Louisville Sluggers with trademarks worn off, among the plastic gallon jugs of Prestone antifreeze and windshield washer, among the rusted garden tools, among the misshapen leather cleats he'd never fit into anymore, their stiffened toes squashed like bullfrogs on a highway.

We're not boys any longer—haven't been for a long time—but I could sense an enthusiasm, a wonder in my friend's voice when he spoke of the cap. I could tell that the cap, if he could only locate it, would be a more treasured possession than anything money could buy. It occurred to me that a young boy's baseball cap, after a few years of wearing, somehow becomes one with the skull.

For a few minutes, our voices spanned halfway across the country. We tried to catch up on our lives, but it was hard to put it all into words. How many years had it been since we played ball? we asked each other as we talked. A decade? Two? How long since we'd even *seen* each other? Neither one of us could remember for sure.

We didn't know it, but that night after we talked, we both crawled back into the farthest, cramped corners of our attics and basements and garages, searching. We were both on our hands and knees, digging through musty boxes, oil-stained boxes, boxes with centipedes scurrying across the bent flaps. All we hoped for was a glimpse of the tops of our old hats flattened into small oval pools. Instead, feeling a little lost, we both returned to the house with torn knees and smudged elbows, a fine dust on our fingertips. The invisible spiderwebs still clung to our faces, spiderwebs we couldn't seem to wipe off.

For days afterward, I thought about our old baseball caps—we always wore red-and-blue Milwaukee Braves caps with the large white *M* in front. I recalled how, after we played for hours in the July heat, we'd sit on the third-base bench of the high school field and stare into the caps, as if there were answers somewhere inside those soaked blue bowls of cloth. We'd stare and watch the cloth slowly lighten in color as the sweat evaporated. On the way home, as the breeze kicked up dusty whirlwinds that rose off the infield and disappeared somewhere above the diamond, we'd spin the caps on our fingertips.

If we had those first ball caps now, we'd study them as if we were craniologists, examine the faint white concentric rings of salt around the edges, rings that circle away, come back, then circle away again. Like the inside of a tree, each ring represents another year of growth, another year of running toward the quickly fading mirage of the major leagues, another year of sweat and desire evaporating into the huge blue overturned cap of the sky.

* * *

Last summer, walking across an empty field after work one day, I discovered an old baseball cap tumbling in the wind, its navy color so faded it appeared whitish gray, its fabric worn so thin from the elements that, when I picked it up, it collapsed flat in my palm. As I stood there, I couldn't help but wonder: Who left it there? What person was so careless to let the wind steal his cap, then never bother to retrieve it as it tumbled across the grass? Why did he give up the game?

Tonight, two weeks after our first conversation, my friend calls again.

The first thing he tells me is that he found his original baseball cap in his attic. "I just reached into a box and it was there," he says, "like magic." He says he might even bring it to our high school reunion when he flies back this summer. I admit to him that I misplaced my cap years ago.

"That's okay," he exclaims. "I've got *two* of them, and I'll give you one. *It's yours.*"

When I hang up the phone, I picture the two of us next summer, crossing our hometown high school baseball field, sipping bottles of beer, spinning our old caps on our index fingers. Neither of us will remember how long it's been, but we'll talk about the years that have passed like so many yellowed pages of newspapers cartwheeling in the wind across center field.

Sitting on the cleat-scratched bench along the third-base line, we'll stare into the caps, blue and faded as our past, and count the rings inside, and perhaps it will all come back to us. Then, with a laugh, we'll stand, and pull the hats on, hoping they still fit.

The Certain Pull
Toward Evening

He'll tell you he's the kind of ballplayer who likes to go to the field in the early evening, when the sun settles among the tips of the pines at the west end of the outfield. Some people play in the middle of the afternoon, at two or three o'clock, but he doesn't like the heat of the day that makes the acid sweat slide from his forehead and burn his eyes, he doesn't like the glare of the bright sky that seems to swallow the fly balls. He'll tell you he likes to have the sun off to one side, red and magnified and easy to glance toward, if you want to.

As he walks onto the field with his young son, their baseball equipment in hand, he pauses a moment and stares at the pines: They're silhouettes now, flat black spires that line the far edge of the field. He can almost hear his father's words from years ago: *Always take the time to look and see what's around you. If you just focus on the baseball, you might miss the beauty of the whole field.*

He'll tell you he doesn't like playing ball in towns closed in by canyons or mountains. He once lived in a western town built along a river basin with canyon walls on both sides. The town's baseball field—its outfield eroded to gravel with a few sharp weeds stabbing through—was a place that lost the light about five o'clock. Long before the sun actually set, it slid behind the tall canyon wall and the park was immersed in shadow as if ink had been spilled across it. Dusk came early, and he felt closed in. Night is premature enough as it is, he's always thought. Why is it that night always seems to be waiting at the edge of day like some dark, hungry beast? He smelled the dry heat from the jagged rocks and the canyon wall, which, no matter where he looked, seemed to cut off his vision.

Yes, if you asked, he'll tell you he likes the broad, flat fields of the plains, the lush greenness. You can throw your sight a long way and it just keeps going. He likes a place where, as the sun begins to set, he can smell the moistness rising out of the earth again, he can smell the first buds of dew on the tips of the grass, grass that, like an endless dream, stretches all the way to the outfield and beyond.

And he likes it that the air is stiller in the evening. The restless breezes of the day abruptly fall to their knees, and without the wind pushing on it, the ball flies true. Most people notice wind on their skin, but once the wind has stopped, they don't think about it anymore. But he actually *feels* the calmness, a sensation in itself on the bare skin of his arms.

This field where he and his son stand tonight could go on forever, too, if it wasn't for the row of jagged pines that cut it off in the distance. Still, it comforts him to know that, beyond the pause of trees, the field continues.

"Dad?" his son calls to him, pulling him from his meditations. "What are you looking at? Let's play."

He pulls a baseball and their gloves from the duffel bag and they play for half an hour. He loves to watch the boy catch his looping throws, loves to see the boy throw them back, to see the baseball rise out of the low shadows of the trees and ignite in the light for a second before it falls back to shadowy earth. He believes that, with his old glove, he could actually catch the last rays of sunlight in his palm. He loves the way his son improves week by week. His catches are smoother, he shows more range as he dashes to his left for a ball that's sinking. Sons grow and improve every day, he thinks. But fathers? What about fathers?

He knows he will be asleep soon; this small town will be asleep soon, buttery lights inside the houses will click off, and the windows will turn opaque like slate. He knows that even as he plays ball this evening, he's already drifting toward sleep, and that sleep is creeping closer toward him. But he doesn't care.

"Dad," his son calls. "Throw the ball back. What are you always staring at?"

He shrugs. Then he says, "Maybe we should go pretty soon."

"Just one more throw," his son pleads. "Just one more."

"Sure," he says.

Later, the boy's words will echo in his mind when he lies down for sleep; they'll keep echoing until his mind is wrapped in shadow: *Just one more.*

At his job, he works with papers: sheets of paper, stacks of papers, file drawers full of papers. His fingers sting with paper cuts. He opens his office door to an avalanche of white that's deep enough to bury any human. A fellow worker once joked, *This job'll make you old fast.*

Lately, a few coworkers who know he plays baseball have started calling him The Kid. It's a nickname that seems to fit him—even if he's wearing a suit and tie, it's as though he's still wearing his Little League uniform. Sometimes his coworkers forget his age. It's the nickname, he thinks. Sometimes, for a while, even *he* forgets his own age.

* * *

One day last year, standing alone in the middle of his small town field at dusk, he had the strangest sensation. He sensed that old ballplayers were sleeping beneath the moist grass. Somehow he could feel them, hundreds of them, beneath his cleats—famous ballplayers, Hall of Famers from his son's picture books, minor leaguers and town ballplayers and unknown guys who never made it, all sleeping just an inch or two beneath the grass. That night he dreamed they all rose after midnight—each player bent from the waist, sat up, and looked around. Then they climbed to their feet, stood on the field, and stared longingly at the place where the sun would rise in a few hours. He saw them holding vigil there, not moving, just staring into the east, waiting. Then, the moment the curved tip of the sun appeared, they lay back down, as if satisfied that the day had returned and life could begin again. Baseball could be played again, and they could gaze up at the bottoms of the kids' tennis shoes caressing the field.

When he woke the next morning, he thought about how maybe he'd be there some day, sleeping with them beneath that field, waiting for midnight so he could rise and peer silently into the distance of the horizon and keep the vigil for the first light.

Yes, he's one who likes to play ball in the evening, just before sunset. Tonight the air is so still he can feel it surrounding him, buoying him off the ground like a thick liquid as he takes a diving leap for the final throw from his son. He catches the ball, tumbles and rolls, but doesn't get up. He lies on his back, the first moisture on the grass blades tingling the back of his neck. He lies there a few seconds, stretching the moment, until his son calls to him. "Nice catch, Dad." His son hesitates, then asks, "Dad, you okay?"

He smiles but doesn't answer, because he knows he doesn't need to talk or even mutter "Sure." He just bends at the waist, sits up, and gazes for a while into his son's eyes, watching the boy's face ignite in the clear, bright shafts of the last slanting light. Then he shifts his vision beyond his son, beyond the sharp black silhouette of the trees at the far end of the field, to the place where the sun lowers itself, an arching bridge of red spreading above it. His son follows his gaze, turns, and stands there, staring and transfixed, as if finally understanding what his father has been seeing all these years.

Where the Old
Ballplayers Go

My son and I turn page after page in the baseball card album, and I'm amazed at how easily our fingers span across the years. On one page, we see the shiny new cards of the nineties, then we've skipped to the eighties and seventies, and finally, on the last few pages, we're all the way back to the sixties and fifties. We slide a few of the oldest cards out of their plastic pockets. These cards are creased, and round-cornered, the cards that have long since lost their gloss, the cards whose colors have faded like the wings of butterflies kept pinned to a board for years. Though I collected these cards in my childhood, I'm not even sure who some of these players are, or what ever became of them. For a moment, I almost expect the cards to crumble in my fingertips.

"This one looks like Grandpa," my son says, pointing to a player with a receding hairline. "Doesn't it?"

"Yeah, a little," I say.

"Who is it?" he asks.

I peer at the face of some player who's been forgotten by time and the record books, some player who was probably good, and consistent at the game, but never a star. "Just some old ballplayer," I say.

"Where do you think he is now?" he asks.

"I have no idea," I admit.

For some reason, my son likes the older cards as much as the current ones. It doesn't matter that they're nearly thirty years old already and he's never seen the players on television. Sometimes I notice him, alone in his room at night, paging through the collection of cards that I bought for a nickel a pack in a creaking-floor Woolworth's and kept in my father's Swisher Sweets cigar box.

A half hour before, in the small ball field down the street, I pitched a few baseballs to my son. He just turned eight this spring, and he always stands close to home, eager, confidently crossing his Louisville Slugger over the plate before each pitch just like the pros do. Nervous about hitting him, I kept the ball low and outside the strike zone; I crept closer to him as I pitched until I stood only thirty feet away.

When I finally tossed one over the center of the plate, he swung hard, cracked a line drive right at me. I moved my glove in front of my chest to block the liner, but the ball skimmed off my wrist and bounced into left center.

Now, as I point to a prize '57 Hank Aaron card, my son notices the purple-red mark on my left wrist where the line drive struck me.

"Does it hurt?" my son asks, a tinge of guilt in his voice.

"Not much," I answer.

He peers at it closely, then says, "I can see the stitch marks from the ball."

I glance at my wrist. I know, from experience in Little League, that I'll carry those stitch marks around with me for a few days before they fade.

"Sorry I hit you," he says.

"That's okay," I say. "It was a good line drive."

"Yeah. But I should have hit it somewhere else."

I shake my head. "Nobody can aim a hit exactly where they want it to go."

We page through a few more cards in silence. When he lifts one page out of the ring binder and holds it in front of his face, the cards, suspended inside their plastic pockets, seem to float. He moves them closer to the light and they become almost transparent.

"Who's this?" he asks, pointing at one card.

"Roger Maris."

"Was he good?"

"Good? He beat Babe Ruth's home run record in sixty-one," I tell him.

"Oh, that's right," he says. I can tell by the way he half-closes his right eye that, inside his head, he's walking back through the rooms of musty baseball stories I've told him the past few years. "Wouldn't it be neat to get his autograph on this card?" he asks.

"I'm afraid we couldn't do that," I say.

"Why not?" he asks.

"Because he's dead."

"Oh," he says, his voice falling.

We gaze at Maris's wide smile on the '61 card, his face caught in time inside the ring binder of our collection, his mid-career stats listed on the back of the card as if he could pick up a bat tomorrow.

"Is Babe Ruth still alive?" my son asks.

"No," I answer. "He died before I was even born."

After a thoughtful pause, my son asks, "Where do ballplayers go when they die? I mean, do they get to play baseball up there?" He waits for an answer. In that moment his eyes are a blue that seems almost too bright.

"I'm not sure," I say.

* * *

After dinner I page through the family photo album, searching for pictures to take to a high school reunion. Suddenly I come upon a creased black-and-white photograph of a young man dressed in a baseball uniform. I pull the photo out and study it.

"That was Grandpa, right?" my son says, looking over my shoulder.

"Right," I reply.

In the picture, my father is about eighteen, still some fifty years from his death.

My mind rushes back to that time my father taught me to hit when I was a boy. I see him after work, standing in the small field, still dressed in dark slacks and his pale yellow shirt with the sleeves rolled. He said, not necessarily to me, but aloud: "I never have time for this." He slid out of his dress shoes, then, with thumb and forefinger, pulled on the toes of his thin gray socks, which clung to his pale feet like leeches until they finally snapped off and floated to the grass.

"Why don't you hit me a couple today?" he said.

"Okay," I said hesitantly. I'd never tried hitting fly balls to anybody—I was only seven, and so far, I'd only hit the easy, underhanded pitches he'd tossed straight to my bat.

He stubbed out his Swisher Sweet cigar on the aluminum post of the backstop, borrowed my glove, too small for his hand, and stood near the worn patch in the grass we called second base, his feet glowing white beneath the cuffs of his pants.

I tapped my Little League bat on home plate and flipped the ball into the air in front of me. I swung and swung, and each time the ball fell with a thump at my feet. I pictured his big, powerful swing, hitting towering pop-ups across the field that sometimes bounded through the gaps in the wood-slat fence and onto the neighbor's back lawn, and I thought *I'll never learn to hit like he can. Never.* Frustrated after about twenty misses, I swung once more with a mighty uppercut. The bat pulled me off balance and I fell onto the hard-packed, grainy dirt of the batter's box, scraping my elbow. The next thing I knew he was leaning over me, reaching down and lifting me to my feet. With the cuff of his shirt, he dabbed the blood from the scrape on my elbow. Then, without a word, he stood behind my back and slid his arms around me.

With arms twice the size of mine, he coached me on how to time my swing, and as he did I inhaled the smell of Old Spice and cigar smoke, tinged with the scent of sweat from his shirt. He cupped his hand beneath my hand and guided it as I tossed the ball into the air. "Not too high," he said, "not too low. Steady. That's the secret. And always keep your swing level." I felt the rough caress of his stubbled cheek against the tender side of my neck.

He stood barefoot in the field again a few minutes later, clapping my mitt on the side of his leg.

Timing it just right like he told me, I swung, hit one that looped over his head.

He never moved for it, just stood with his hands on his hips and watched with a smile as the ball sailed beyond him and landed in the outfield. He jogged out to the ball, rolled it toward me, and loped back to his position near second. I hit another one over his head, then another. Though they kept flying over his head, he never moved any deeper. "I think you're getting it," he said with a grin as he stood panting, hands on his knees, "but do you have to make your old man work so hard?"

Ten years later, when I was in high school, my father and I strolled to the athletic field. His waistline carried the baggage of middle age, and we hadn't played baseball for years, but that day I asked him to hit some fly balls to me so I could practice for the varsity tryouts.

I waited deep in center as he tossed the ball up, swung, and missed. After about a dozen swings, he tapped a couple of weak grounders that didn't even reach me; then he missed the ball several more times. Finally he shuffled toward me, shaking his head, dragging the barrel of the bat behind him in the grass.

"That's enough," he said to me through puffed, red cheeks. "Guess I've lost it."

"Can I look at this for a minute?" my son asks, pulling my father's old photo from my fingers.

"Go ahead," I say.

I watch him studying the photo, holding it up close to his face. "He sure is young in this picture," my son says. "He looks like a boy."

Tonight I walk past my son's doorway, see him alone in his room. Propped on his thin arms beneath his bedside lamp, he pages through the decades of old cards.

It's well past his bedtime, so I poke my head into the doorway. "What are you doing?" I ask.

"I'm just looking at the old guys," he says.

I pat him on the head, slip the album from his fingers. "It's late," I say. "Better get some sleep."

Then I notice something sliding out from between the pages, a picture too big to fit in the plastic pockets.

It's the picture of my father in his baseball uniform.

"Did you put this in here?" I ask him.

"Yeah." He nods. "He belongs there."

* * *

Downstairs, I find myself opening the album beneath a lamp to browse through the old cards. I glance at my elbow, wondering if I can still see the scar from years ago, but it's healed and gone.

Before I fall asleep, I lie in bed and think about my son's question earlier that afternoon. I don't know where old ballplayers go when they die. I used to think they go to a gigantic major league stadium, where they walk slowly to their position in the infield or the outfield wearing a new uniform. They notice the velvety texture of the new-mown grass as they step lithely across it with their polished, cleated shoes. Then they stand there, taking a deep breath of the endless summer air, raising their hands to wave at the grandstands full of cheering fans.

But now I think differently. I watch my son, sleeping peacefully in his bed, and I want to tell him old ballplayers don't go to a fancy stadium full of people. The fame and the cheering crowd aren't what's important. Perhaps, in a moment as quick as the turning of a page, the old ballplayers find themselves walking barefoot in a small field in a town where they grew up. They're wearing everyday clothes. The grass of the field is unmown between the worn patches of dirt, and the wood-slat fence that surrounds it is broken and leaning. But none of that matters. What matters is that the old ballplayers are stepping effortlessly from the outfield toward the batter's box.

What matters is that when they reach home, they lean over and gaze into the eyes of their small son or daughter who has fallen to the hard ground. What matters is they slide their arms around their children and gently lift them back to their feet.

Keeping Time

Sometimes the human heart is the only clock in the world that keeps true time.

Coach John Brace, a pile of team jerseys on his arm, leaned rhythmically left, then right, like a pendulum between the two rows of wooden benches. As he walked down the aisle of that high school locker room, Coach tossed jerseys to the boys he'd chosen for the freshman baseball team after a day of tryouts. I sat in my gym shorts at the end of the bench, the varnished wood sticky and cool beneath my thighs, and though it wasn't cold in the room, shivers rushed outward from the middle of my spindly body like ripples from the center of a pond. I felt as though I'd been sitting on that bench all my life, waiting for that one moment. As Coach rocked closer, I remember watching the blue-and-gold jerseys fluttering, in slow motion, to the outstretched hands of each boy, and praying my hands would be next.

I had practiced tirelessly for that one day of tryouts—I knew it would be my first chance to make a real baseball team. Sometimes, alone in a field behind a warehouse, I bounced a ball off the brick wall and fielded grounders. Sometimes, dropping quarters into the slot, I'd swing and swing in a batting cage until my shoulder muscles ached. But more often than not, during the summer days of seventh and eighth grades, I practiced with my best friend, Steve Lyon, at the old West School field until our crew cuts glistened with sweat. "Sheese, we're improving," Steve often mused afterward as we sat beneath the shade of a billowing elm. "There's no way we won't make the team, man."

One day, after our usual routine of batting practice, I was goofing around in the outfield with my ball cap on sideways; I jumped and shook my arms in the air and howled at the sky as Steve watched, laughing. In the middle of my act, Steve cut the laughter, then pointed subtly with his thumb and I looked behind me. My whole body went numb when I saw Coach Brace in his powder-blue Dodge, watching me from the stoplight. Coach lifted one hand politely to wave to us as he drove off. Upset for the rest of that afternoon, I kept repeating to Steve how ridiculous I must have looked to the man who'd be our baseball coach next year. I knew Coach Brace was serious about baseball, and I cursed my luck that he'd driven by when I was acting stupid instead of when I was hitting a liner over third base or making one of my patented diving catches. I told Steve how I didn't look like a ballplayer but like some clowning kid who didn't care. "Don't worry," Steve assured me, "he'll never remember."

For Career Day in civics class that fall, leaning over my narrow-ruled paper, I scrawled an essay about how I planned to be a major league baseball player. Beneath the bright spotlight of my cone-shaped desk lamp, I wrote that I'd sign a pro baseball contract after high school, play a while in the minor leagues—maybe in nearby Madison or Wausau—then be called up to the majors. As I described each step of my career, the words flowed as easily as players running onto the field at the start of a game. To me, the logic and the progression of the essay seemed so simple, so undeniably true. When I was finished, I printed the title in tall, bold letters at the top: TOMORROW. At school the next morning, the civics teacher, Mrs. Griswald, handed the essay back to me, saying I had written it in pencil and I was supposed to write it in pen. Mrs. Griswald also jotted at the bottom of the essay, in red marker: *What if you* don't *make it???* As I recopied the essay that night with a black Bic pen, I remember thinking to myself, *I'll make it. I will make it.*

In the locker room after freshman tryouts, we waited on the benches while Coach Brace unlocked the supply room. Somehow, nervous as I felt, I was still aware of the scents in the room: the smell of must and the dank cement floor of the shower, the smell of leather where boys' palms had sweated into their gloves, the faint odor of the damp, loamy April earth tracked in by our cleated shoes.

Coach reappeared with the jerseys and gave a brief speech. He was known throughout the high school and our town as a gentle man, and a great teacher, and he had a reputation for these inspirational speeches, but I was feeling too much anxiety to listen: All I could hear was the soft slapping of water dripping from the showerheads, a sound that seemed to grow louder until it nearly exploded in my ears. Then Coach stepped down the aisle, handing out the jerseys. He leaned left, then right as if he were dancing a slow waltz.

By the time Coach reached the end of the bench where Steve and I and a couple of other guys waited, only two jerseys were draped over his wrist. Coach hesitated a moment, tossed one jersey to Steve. Then he turned and tossed the second one to a boy who sat across from me.

With that tossed jersey, which I can still see now, a blue-and-gold blur floating softly in the air, the coach threw a young boy's dreams out a locker-room window, and they spiraled miles and miles to the hard ground.

I don't remember what Coach said after that. He might have been saying, "Boys, I'm really sorry," but the loud pain filling my skull blocked out his words.

Walking home with Steve, I couldn't help feeling an anger for Coach Brace, a kind of hatred growing steadily inside me, spreading to every artery and muscle and nerve. I'd never hated anyone before, but in my mind, Coach Brace became meaner and more vindictive by the second. I swore at him, I called him names, I did cruel imitations of his locker-room speeches.

"You got screwed, man," Steve said, trying to make me feel better. "Plain and simple. You *deserve* to be on that team. You're better than *all* those guys who got jerseys."

I stopped in the middle of the sidewalk and glared at Steve. "Including you, I suppose."

Steve glanced down at the jersey folded on his duffel bag, then back at me. "Yeah," he said. "Including me."

His words didn't help. My world was changing at that moment; nothing could stop it from pivoting away from my future as a baseball player. Nothing could lighten the enormous disappointment that crushed me like a weight. I swore I'd never speak to Coach Brace again.

When we reached my front door, Steve uttered our usual farewell. "Tomorrow," he said.

"Yeah," I said feebly, unable to lift my gaze from the concrete. "Tomorrow."

After supper I pulled my civics class essay from my desk drawer, walked to the corner of the backyard, lit a match, and burned those pages one by one. I watched my looping words darken as the paper curled in on itself like a fist. The ashes fell onto the worn spot in the dirt where home plate used to be.

I never tried out for the baseball team the next three years of high school, even though Steve said I should. I was too hurt, and just couldn't face Coach Brace for another tryout. Steve played well, a star third baseman during our four years of high school, and the team won the conference championship one year. After school on spring days, Steve stopped at his locker next to mine; he pulled his books out quickly, and I knew, as usual, he was headed to baseball practice.

"What's up tonight, buddy?" he asked me once after seventh period.

"Nothing." I shrugged, clicking my locker door shut, then opening it, then clicking it shut again.

"Man, I wish I had your free time," he said.

"I wish I had your practice," I replied.

Suddenly awkward in his untucked madras shirt and white Levi's, Steve pretended to adjust the cover on his science book. We both knew my being cut from the team created a kind of chasm between us, and neither of us was too comfortable talking about it. Then, before he turned, he gave me a quick grin, nodded, and said, "Tomorrow."

I nodded back as he hurried down the hall toward the locker room. Some afternoons I loitered in the empty hallway until the team took the field and began their warm-up exercises. Through the high, distorted glass of the second-story window, I watched the players wavering in the distance. As those four years passed, I decided it was a stupid, small idea of mine, anyway, to want to be a major leaguer. After all—what were my chances?

Twenty years later, when I returned to town for a high school reunion, someone said that Coach Brace had become seriously ill with cancer. The rumors circulated among my classmates that Coach, who had been our senior class advisor, would try to make it to the gathering that night, but everyone said he looked very bad, the illness eating away at him. Some of my classmates shook their heads and said his chances weren't good.

When Coach Brace walked into the reunion amid a flurry of handshakes and friendly calls from former students, his face looked as though the skin had collapsed inward onto the bone, and shadows, like dark gray bunting, clung to the skin beneath his eyes. I turned toward him as he made his way through the crowd, and then, when the old hurt rose inside me, I turned away.

After the reunion dinner, Coach stepped to the microphone in the high school gym, his navy blue suit jacket seeming too large for him. During a short speech, he bowed his head slightly, lowered his voice, and told us the illness had been tough on him. "But I'm going to beat this thing," he said, raising his head. "I'm going to beat it. If baseball taught me one thing, it taught me not to give up."

After the speeches, Coach spotted me standing by the makeshift bar in the corner of the gym; he walked over and greeted me. We exchanged small talk for a few minutes, and while we talked, I couldn't stop that locker-room scene from replaying in my mind.

Then, out of nowhere, Coach said, "You always were a good ballplayer. I remember that. I remember seeing you and Steve Lyon practicing by the old West School." He toasted me with his plastic cup of punch. "You guys were always a great addition to my team," he said proudly.

To my team. I was stunned by those last words, and a sudden realization hit me: Coach Brace *never even remembered* cutting me from the team. That moment, which had meant so much to me, that moment I'd carried around for years inside my stomach like a huge, undissolved stone had simply disappeared from his mind. To him, I was just one of his former players who contributed to those conference championship teams. I thought about correcting him, telling him *No, I never played on your team. You cut me, remember?* Thought about telling how because of him, I went home that night and lay for hours in my unlit room, my future abruptly turned to ashes. Instead, I looked into Coach's eyes and what I saw there was the kindness I'd refused to acknowledge all those years. Then I began to visualize his illness—the cancer spreading its gray, deadly branches just beneath his skin.

"So," he said, erasing my vision, "do you still play ball?"

"Yeah," I replied. "Sometimes. With a few older guys, I mean."

He chuckled, grinned benignly. "That's the wonderful thing about baseball. You're never too old." He paused, then added solemnly, "When you've got baseball in your life, you're always a winner. Don't forget that."

His words reverberated in my head and I closed my eyes. I realized that these were the same words he'd spoken to us after the freshman tryouts in the locker room. I had the dizzying sensation that, without realizing it, I was walking on some wide, cyclical path, and I'd just passed a starting point again. I opened my eyes, and, for the first time, I understood those words. "I won't forget," I said.

Coach and I shook hands. Before he turned to leave, he caught me off guard by sliding his arm around me and giving me a hug. His frail hand clapped the back of my shoulder, and in those few seconds all the hurt feelings seemed to slide out of my body, rise through the blue and gold crepe paper wafting over our heads, drift through the ceiling of the high school gym, and evaporate into the endless night sky. My pain, which I'd always considered so enormous, suddenly seemed very small to me; I wondered how I could possibly have carried it for so long.

Later, as Coach walked toward the exit, I knew it might be the last time I'd ever see him. But then, I thought, maybe not. Maybe he'd be there, standing at the podium the next time we got together.

During the reunion, Steve and I talked for a while, but the evening passed too quickly, and we never got around to mentioning our ballplaying days. At one A.M. I said farewell to my classmates as we shuffled into the entryway of the gym. I glanced around to find Steve, but I couldn't spot him in the crowd.

Standing by the car with my wife, I heard a voice call to me from behind. "Hey, man," the voice said. "Wanna play some baseball?"

I turned to see Steve leaning against his car, mitt in one hand, beer in the other.

"You mean here?" I gasped. "Now?"

"Why not?"

I glanced at my wife, who smiled and nodded at me. Opening the car trunk, I pulled out my old glove.

Steve and I set down our cans of beer, slipped off our suit jackets, and draped them on posts at the edge of the parking lot. We stood beneath the glow of the full moon, awkward in our white shirts and ties, our waists a little thicker, our hair thinner and grayer, the cells inside our bodies subtly changing second by second. We tossed the ball across the open stretch of black asphalt. It wasn't the best playing surface, we agreed with a laugh as the soles of our shined shoes scuffed across it, but it would do for now. Though neither of us said it, Steve and I knew what each of us was thinking: Tomorrow we'd go to the old West School field, where we used to practice, and we'd play baseball. We'd slip into our worn spikes, torn T-shirts, and faded caps and play baseball. And if the field was gone, then we'd play in the place where it *used* to be. Tomorrow.

That night, in the diffused light, the ball seemed to flutter toward our outstretched gloves. I listened to the rhythmic beat of the ball in the leather pockets. The thought crossed my mind that you could keep time by a game of catch, this heartbeat, this throwing back and forth, back and forth, each swing of the arm like the sweep of a pendulum, each throw another year. It was then that I heard the honk of a horn, and in that instant, time stopped.

We turned to see Coach Brace, idling in his old powder-blue Dodge, watching us from the far end of the lot, lifting his hand in a wave.

SIX

Into
the
Wind

Hitting into
the Wind

As I step into the batter's box again, I remember my
father saying, "Each time up might be your last." He understood that rule, and I do, too. This might be my last chance
to connect with the ball, to send a small, round piece of
myself out there toward the cyclone fence. The game is tied
in the ninth inning; two outs, no one on base. The pitcher
leers at me, then looks for his sign. He'd give anything to see
me die up there at the plate. But I imagine the ball rising from
my bat to left field, cutting through the blue air to its height,
tracing a perfect bridge in the sky as it begins its slow, lazy
descent back toward earth, toward green bleachers.

I know the meaning of the home run. It's the slow circling
of the bases, and then the return. I know it well. My father
was a traveling salesman, with the highway wrapped around
his wrist like a gray sweatband. My mother and brother and
I understood that we were the bases he loved, the bases he
touched gently, briefly, with the edge of his big, soft foot. We
learned early about his game—the round trip toward home:
the going away, the coming back. We learned that he'd stay
with us in the house for a few days, and then the phone would

ring, startling the air. From behind the cyclone fence in back, we'd watch him drive off. The silence fell like a tarpaulin across our yard.

My mother felt his leaving more than anyone; she always worried that he might fall asleep at the wheel during those long driving days. She'd sit on her knees, motionless in the grass, staring at nothing through the diamond shapes in the fence. I'd lean into that fence, pressing my face against the crisscrossed wires until they left lines on my cheeks.

Now I dig into the sand of the batter's box with my cleats and stare at the fence I haven't hit today, though I've been at bat three times. So far, I'm nobody at the plate. Nobody. The pitcher takes his time out there, rotating the ball behind his back, tightening his face, tightening his fingers on the seams, trying to squeeze some magic into leather.

I stare at those other minor league players on the field. I recognize that wild look in their eyes. It's a coiled look—the face is a watch spring. It's a look that says I can see far beyond the walls and grandstands of this ballpark, far beyond this little town. A look that says I can see all the way to the majors.

Just make contact, my dad used to say when I was in Little League. Contact will get you where you want to go.

The pitcher winds up and fires the ball from a pretzel of arms and legs. It's a curve. I let it go. The ball pops into the catcher's mitt; a globe of dust puffs out. I feel the wind on my face.

"Strike one," the umpire barks.

2

For nearly twenty years, my father traveled the highways in search of sales. He mounted a plastic compass on the dash of our car and the red needle bobbed in the liquid as he drove, selling bronze-plated children's banks. Once he gave me a bank from the boxes he kept stacked in the deep, wide trunk of his Oldsmobile. Everyone needs to save for the future, he used to say; a company like this will never go out of business. I kept that miniature Model T Ford—half full of pennies—on my dresser.

Those early days he used to worry about falling asleep at the wheel; sometimes it seemed that falling asleep was his greatest enemy. During one stretch, he had to drive four hundred or five hundred miles a day for a week. After that, he told us, just thinking about getting behind the wheel made him drowsy and gave him a backache.

Mom told him maybe it was better he was in pain, because then he wouldn't fall asleep so easily. Sometimes, at dinner, he'd describe how he fought it. I used to imagine how he'd turn the car radio up loud, the warbling voices of girls on the commercials blaring until his ears hurt. He kept fighting it, drumming on the steering wheel until the feeling passed, or stretching his mouth wide as if he were cheering a long home run.

It was the repetition, he said. Repetition killed everything. Whenever I pictured him driving, I pictured him on the same road every morning, falling asleep, resting his head on the padded dash.

Sometimes, when he got home from a sales trip, the first thing he'd do was take me to the sandlot field across the street. I'd pause behind the backstop, fingers curled tightly into the wires, and watch him crouch close to the wooden home plate. To me, he looked like some kind of baseball hero, though his hair was thinning and he still wore his white long-sleeved shirt and gray flannel slacks. I heard the joints in his back crack as he dragged the bat around with a grunt and hit fly balls to me. Before he quit, he told me to move aside, and he tried to drive the balls toward the line of scrub trees beyond the snow fence at the edge of the field. But the ball never landed where it should have—it rose high and long, but always seemed to die, tugged back toward home plate by the strong Iowa winds gusting off the flatlands.

Afterward, we walked back toward the house, his arm around my bony shoulders. His black wingtip shoes, caked with dust, never wiped clean as he shuffled through the first long growth of spring grass.

I learned a rule to live by: Always hit with the wind.

"Those hits would have gone a lot farther," he said to me, "if it wasn't for the wind. A lot farther."

3

Now that I'm older, I have a wife, a son, and a game of my own. Sometimes I have to leave the ones I love for a while. I start the car, my duffel bag packed in the trunk, new base-balls clustered inside like eggs. I drive to a place where the grass is perfectly groomed, where the wind leans toward center, where, the moment I step onto the field, the diamond seems to light up for me.

As I wait for the next pitch, I sink my toes into the silky sand of the batter's box. I just need that one hit, I tell myself, as the pitcher glares and tucks in his already tucked-in shirt. I want to hit a ball so hard it will turn to pure light.

I watch the pitcher and the other fielders, and I realize that there is no present for minor leaguers. Here on this field, there's only a past—a long, struggling past—and a major league future. A future vague as the fading white glow above the lights of the scoreboard at night. I realize, as the other players stare, that they hate me. Hate me, not for who I am now, but for who I might become.

* * *

I keep seeing this scene from last week: Driving alone on a county road, I came to a bridge that spanned a small river. The place reminded me of a park where I had picnicked as a child with my father: the sweeping curve of the river, a few scrub pines like brush strokes in the distance, and an old ball field, overgrown with long weeds. It could have been the sandlot field, but I live hundreds of miles from Iowa. I had to pull over on gravel, stop the car, and stare at the scene. The water was high—swollen by spring rains—and the current was strong in the middle, yet the water seemed almost motionless along the banks. Time must move that way, I thought. When you look too closely, you never see anything change.

I watched the scene shrink in the rearview mirror as I drove away, drove nowhere for hours, drove the whole morning. Suddenly, rounding a curve, I saw it again: the same bridge, the same scattered pines, the same deep grass in center field, the same swollen river, moving faster in the middle than near its banks.

When I die, I thought, I will die near a bridge like this. When I die, it will be like dozing off. I'll turn the wheels toward the side of a bridge, and the metal guardrail will open its tender, silvery arms for me. After the soft hit against the clear water, the car will settle slowly to the bottom of the river, and I'll grip the wheel and keep driving at seventy, the front seat filling with water, the silt rising up around the fenders like dust from a county road.

The pitcher fires the second pitch. I'm not ready for it. He's caught me off guard, daydreaming again. The pitch bends over the plate.

"Strike two," the umpire barks.

4

Though I've played this game for years, the same simple things still please me. I love the sound. Yes, the crack of dull leather against wood. I love the way it echoes off fences, off flat faces of houses, off my childhood.

Dad used to talk about the sound he heard each day—the sound of tires on pavement. He claimed he knew, without looking at the speedometer, whether he was going fifty-five or sixty just by the pitch of the whirling tires on asphalt. There were nights, he said, when he'd wake up, alone in a motel, the song of seventy going through his head. He'd sit up and look around, and the sound would fade. Just fade, and become the buzzing of the battered air conditioner.

My father spent a lifetime laying down lines for himself, lines he always tried to follow. But lately I've discovered the truth: Rain will pockmark the smoothest of chalk lines. Wind will blow the whiteness in faint, ghostly gusts across a field. Imperceptible shifts in the earth will make a straight chalk line waver like a mirage in a year or two.

Awake and in his dreams, my father stared at lines through the windshield. They never were straight—the licorice asphalt shifted in the hot sun, the horizon wavered. Far ahead on the highway, heat collected in great pools of water he never seemed to reach.

The morning after he learned his company was going bankrupt, he stood behind his car, staring into the trunk. He picked up box after box, unwrapping the bronze banks from layers of tissue paper—the kind they pack around new baseballs. Suddenly he reared back and hurled one bank across the yard; it landed silently in the tall weeds at the edge of the woods.

"If it wasn't for the damned wind, it would have gone a lot farther. A lot farther."

5

I step back into the batter's box and look to the bleachers in left. Unless there's a fence, the long fly balls are useless. I need something to aim toward besides the endless horizon. Dad once said, as he gazed toward the line of scrub trees, "What good is a long fly ball if there's no fence to judge it?"

6

That day in April, it finally happened. My father fell asleep at the wheel. *He just fell asleep,* my mother gasped over and over after she pressed the telephone onto its cradle. As I stood there, waiting for her to explain, I pictured him, alone on some highway, letting the steering wheel go, slumping into the front seat, the car veering toward the killing ditch.

7

I'll always remember that day in April. After he fell asleep, Dad rose to the steering wheel, resurrected. Bruised, but not badly hurt, he awoke. The car was still idling in the ditch, exhaust filling the inside like some invisible, deadly water. He grabbed the steering wheel again, rolled down the window, and accelerated; the bent wheels just spun, mud slapping against the undersides of the fenders. He told us later that the speedometer read seventy, but the car never moved an inch. The needle of that plastic dashboard compass just rocked in the liquid. It was a story he liked to retell over the years, though Mom hated to hear it and often retreated to the kitchen. He'd clap his thick palms softly together to imitate the sound of that slapping mud. The speedometer read seventy, he'd say with a chuckle, but the car never moved an inch.

8

Mom sensed the hour and minute Dad would arrive home from a sales trip. She walked out the door, sat alone on the screened porch, and waited, swaying back and forth on a card-table chair. Suddenly she turned her whole body toward the hill, where the silver hood ornament of his car would appear. The Oldsmobile seemed to rise slowly from the asphalt as it climbed the subtle grade lined with fences.

At first, no one made a sound. Then our whole house resonated. Applause filled every cupboard, every closet, every ear. He was a man rounding third after a grand slam, and we leapt to our feet and danced to the front yard to greet him.

He pulled himself slowly from the car, his stocky legs stiff, and limped toward us for a hug.

9

The grandstands seem empty now except for my father. He sits in the front row, his shirt like a white chalk stain against the green paint. He's been watching me all this time, but I never noticed him.

I turn my head toward the mound; the pitcher is beginning his third windup. All he needs now is one swing, to see my bat push uselessly through a pillow of air. I wait. My heart thumps, thumps like the catcher's fist in the pocket of his mitt.

My muscles wake. I lean into the ball. Lean into the wind with my shoulders, my heart. The sound of the bat is right; it resonates in my wrists, in the hollows of my arms, in my chest. I recognize that sound—it's the perfect sound of connection deep in my brain, it's the crackle I felt inside my spine when, on that day in April, a tow truck brought back the dented Oldsmobile, and Dad leaned Mom against the fence and kissed her.

I jog out to the bases, touch each one gently with the edge of my soft foot. By the time I reach second, my legs are stiff, and I'm limping slightly.

As I round third toward home, my father stands, his eyes widening like a child's, and he grips his fingers hard into the diamonds of the backstop as if it's a wheel he fears is turning.

About the Author

Paul Middlestaedt

BILL MEISSNER, who grew up in Iowa and Wisconsin, lives with his wife and son in St. Cloud, Minnesota, where he is director of creative writing at St. Cloud State University. The author of three books of poetry, Meissner is the recipient of five PEN/NEA Syndicated Fiction awards, a Loft-McKnight Award of Distinction for Fiction, and an NEA Creative Writing Fellowship. During the spring and summer, he finds himself on the ball field cracking a few line drives and shagging fly balls in the outfield.

THE WIKI WAY

THE WIKI WAY

Quick Collaboration on the Web

BO LEUF
WARD CUNNINGHAM

ADDISON–WESLEY

Boston • San Francisco • New York • Toronto • Montreal
London • Munich • Paris • Madrid
Capetown • Sydney • Tokyo • Singapore • Mexico City

The publisher offers discounts on this book when ordered in quantity for special sales. For more information, please contact:

Pearson Education Corporate Sales Division
One Lake Street
Upper Saddle River, NJ 07458
(800) 382-3419
corpsales@pearsontechgroup.com

Visit Addison-Wesley on the Web: www.awl.com/cseng/

Library of Congress Cataloging-in-Publication Data
Leuf, Bo.
    The Wiki way: quick collaboration on the Web / Bo Leuf, Ward Cunningham
        p. cm.
    Includes bibliographical references and index.
    ISBN 0-201-71499-X
    1. Wiki (Computer science) I. Cunningham, Ward. II. Title.
TK5105.8882.L48 2001
005.7'2—dc21   00–054280
                                                                    CIP

ISBN 0-201-71499-X
Text printed on recycled paper

1 2 3 4 5 6 7 8 9 10—MA—0504030201
First printing, March 2001

We dedicate this book to the thousands of authors that have made Wiki an interesting place to visit.

—Bo Leuf and Ward Cunningham